RORY FORESMAN

THE
SUPERSTITION
KID

THE LONG ROAD HOME

Copyright laws protect this book, and therefore, no part of it can be used or reproduced in any manner without obtaining written permission from Foresman Publications. Any reproduction, distribution, or adaptation of the material contained within this book without permission is strictly prohibited.

This is a work of fiction inspired by locations in Arizona during the 1800s. Real people mentioned are based on historical information available today, while other characters and names are entirely fictional. Any resemblance to actual people, living or dead, is purely coincidental.

Cover Design by BookCoverZone.com
Book Layout and Sketches by Ryan Foresman

Printed in the United States of America

First edition 2nd printing

Copyright © 2025 Rory Foresman
All rights reserved.

ISBN: 979-8-9906678-5-3

Foresman Publishing
An imprint of Foresman Publications
ForesmanPublications.com

Dedication

To my beloved wife, Rosanne,
and my talented brother,
Ryan, whose editing
support has been invaluable.

I'd like to express my heartfelt
gratitude to the Superior Arizona
Chamber of Commerce, the
Superior Public Library, and the
Bob Jones Museum for their
assistance and encouragement.

Foreward

I AM OFTEN ASKED, "Did this really happen, or was this a real person?" The answer is both yes and no. Most of my novels are Western-based fiction that incorporates historic places, people, and events. Depending on the genre, these books can be difficult to classify. Are they historical fiction or Westerns? The answer is yes; they are both. As I wrote in the Copyright page of the book. *This is a work of fiction inspired by locations in Arizona during the 1800s. Real people mentioned are based on historical information available today, while other characters and names are entirely fictional. Any resemblance to actual people, living or dead, is purely coincidental.*

How can you distinguish between historical fact and fiction? This can be determined by two factors: your historical knowledge and your curiosity. Most people ask me these questions out of curiosity, and I take that as a compliment. I like to think I have a vivid imagination, but I must admit that it's not as great as I would like it to be. When writing a story that incorporates historical information, it can be quite a challenge. It often requires hours of research on related topics. I frequently say that the time spent on research can take as long as writing the book itself.

Addressing these proverbial questions upfront may help satisfy your curiosity about what is true and what is fiction as you read the first book in the Superstition Kid series. If you are not familiar with Arizona, three Old West towns in this story that still exist today: Superior, Florence, and Tucson. The fourth town is Pinal City. A mining town located a few miles west of Superior, where only the ruins of its foundations remain. The 343 acres of the Boyce Thompson Arboretum sit below Pickpost Mountain and on the edge of where Pinel City was once located. The arboretum contains desert plants, hidden gardens, a pond, miles of trails, and historic buildings.

All mountains, creeks, vegetation, and wildlife mentioned can be found in Arizona. In this story, you will encounter various characters, including both historical figures and fictional ones.

In this first book of the Superstition Kid series, Captain George Graham of the British Army became intrigued by the Scottish Deerhound (also known as the Irish Wolfhound) in the early to mid 1800s and starts rescuing the remaining dogs. The next historical character is Ed Schieffelin, the founder of the town of Tombstone, Arizona, famed for being the site of the gunfight involving Wyatt Earp at the O.K. Corral.

Take your time reading this historical fiction Western, and as your curiosity and intellect demand more, consider conducting your own research to learn about the people and places from our past. Finally, be sure to read the "Travel the Book" section at the end of this Western. Visit the ghost towns and historic western towns that hold the untamed frontier spirit, echoing with gunfire in the dusty streets and rugged landscapes of the Old West.

Author, Rory Foresman

Chapter One

Up here, kid," called a voice high up in the rocks. "You got Injuns on yer trail. You'd best get up here before they see you."

The young rider stopped his horse when he heard a voice calling to him. His horse gently pawed at the ground, eager to continue. He tilted his head back to survey the rocky hillside looming above, the sun casting a brilliant glare that made it difficult to see. Raising his hand to shield his eyes from the harsh light, he squinted, hoping to catch a glimpse of the person hidden among the boulders and shrubs.

"Another twenty feet cut through the boulders on yer right. You'll see a game trail. T'll bring ye right up. Hurry now. Don't have much time."

The rider urged his horse forward, guiding it carefully between the rocks. The trail was well concealed, offering a safe route for deer and other wildlife to travel unseen.

"Don't dally," the voice urgently whispered, "they're getting close. Be quiet. Sounds can echo off these here canyon walls. Hurry now."

When the rider reached the summit, he found himself in a spacious cove nestled between large boulders. The man who guided him stood watch among the rocks, armed with a rifle.

"Put your horse back there with mine, he whispered. "Then join me."

The hidden location had been used before, not only by the man who may have saved his life but also by others long before him, as evidenced by the pictographs on the stones around them. The hideaway included a small cave unseen from the trail below. Near the cave entrance water trickled from the rocks into a small pool carved into the stone. Grass and a lone shade tree grew next to it.

Dismounting from his horse, he wrapped the reins around a low branch giving it access to the grass around the stone pool. Here, his horse would be calm and content. He pulled his rifle from its scabbard and grabbed an extra box of ammunition from his saddlebags. Quickly, he moved to the rocks beside the man, watching the trails below. After glancing over the edge, he turned to the man who had led him to this hidden location.

He could tell the man was a gold miner by his dusty, tattered clothing and worn hat. The man's pants were tucked into his boots, and he had a long, gray beard and shaggy hair peeking out from under his hat. Although he looked nearly 80, he was probably in his 50s.

He placed a finger over his lips to signal silence, then pointed down the hill. The young rider peered carefully over the edge and saw riders below—Apaches.

The group wore white men's clothing, military attire, and moccasins on their feet. Some of them had beaded vests and red bandanas tied around their foreheads. Their hair was long; a few individuals had it braided. All members had knives in their belts. Most had bow and arrows, some had rifles.

They watched as the Apache moved slowly, scanning the ground for signs while avoiding the rocky terrain above. Everything they needed to know could be found on the trail. Looking up at the rocky cliffs could draw unwanted fire from a sniper. They kept their eyes down to avoid revealing their location and remaining safe from an ambush.

The two men crouched behind a cluster of rough, jagged rocks, carefully hidden from view. They could see their adversaries moving through the arid landscape from their vantage point, aware of the threat lurking just out of sight. The sun cast harsh shadows, highlighting the intricate patterns of the terrain.

Both men were keenly aware of the Apache's exceptional tracking skills. They understood that these skilled warriors could interpret even the faintest signs of life among the stones and brush. The wind carried whispers of unease; they knew the Apache would quickly figure out how many lurked in the rocky outcrop if they stayed in their position for too long. The atmosphere was charged as they braced for what lay ahead, aware that each second in this perilous game of cat and mouse could be someone's last.

General George Crook had sought the assistance of Apaches a few years earlier to help track down Apache sub-tribes that were still evading capture, refusing to stay on the reservation, and continuing to raid towns and stagecoach lines. He convinced Chiricahua Apache subchief Chato, who had surrendered alongside Cochise in 1872, to become a scout and aid in locating the Chiricahua Apache led by Geronimo. It was unclear whether the Apache warriors below were associated with Geronimo or other tribes in the area, and the two men were not interested in finding out.

The miner cautiously lifted his rifle, aimed between two large rocks, and waited. The kid carefully peeked over the rocky edge. As he did, the Native Apaches stopped their horses at the spot where the kid stepped off the trail. The kid glanced over at the miner, who again put his finger to his lips. They looked down at the spot and spoke to each other. Not once did they look up into the rocks. Moments later, they moved on without incident.

The miner and the kid waited silently, watching for another ten minutes, until the miner stood up.

"You think they know we're up here?" the kid asked the miner.

"Oh, they knew. They always know— we need to be extra careful; they could be part of Geronimo's band."

"I heard he escaped the reservation and was in hiding again."

"Aye, it's true, laddie. I'm gonnae climb higher and get a good look around—doubt they'll be back. If they wanted us, they'd have come for us by now. It's not like them tae backtrack. Make yourself at home. I'll get a fire and some coffee goin' when I get back."

Thirty minutes later, the miner came into the clearing. The kid, resting against his saddle, stood up.

"Sorry to meet ye under these circumstances," the miner said, reaching for the lad's hand and givin' it a firm shake. "Ah'm Angus… Angus Black."

"Nice to meet you," said the kid, "I'm Jacob Long."

"Good to know, kid. Call me Scotty. Don't use Angus much anymore. I don't like it. My parents thought it a cruel joke tae name me Angus. They said it reminded them of the old country, so they named me after a cow in Scotland—a Black Angus. So don't ye tell anyone now!

Call me Scotty. Everyone does, lad—and if'n ye ain't notis,' I have a slight Scottish accent."

"Oh, well, I'm glad you told me; I hadn't noticed," Jacob said with a grin. The miner got a big smile on his face.

Angus got busy with the fire and had a coffee pot steaming on some flat rocks on the fire's edge. Meanwhile, the kid grabbed his tin cup, some dried meat called pemmican, and a couple of pieces of hardtack from his bags. Pemmican is Jerky with bits of fruit, introduced to the early settlers by local natives, and most often made from buffalo and its Tallow. Using Tallow would help preserve the meat.

"Ah, come, come now, have some coffee, lad. If'n yer hungry? I got me some side pork in my packs."

"No, I'm well supplied. Do you need anything? I got some extra coffee grounds," Jacob said as he sipped the coffee Angus had poured.

"Well, now. I might take ye up on that," Angus replied. "So, where ye heading, kid? Just passing through? Haven't seen ye around these parts befur'."

"That's a lot of questions. Don't rightly know where or how to start."

"Sorry, laddie, I don't get tae talk tae people much. Just digging up a conversation, I 'spose."

"It's okay, I understand. My parents moved out here when I was eight—lived a few miles north of here on the edge of the Superstitions. Started ranchin', they did.

"So, yer the Superstition Kid," Scotty grinned.

"You sure do like those nicknames," Jacob replied.

"Sorry, a bad habit I've got into. So, how long have ye been away?"

"Oh, for more than three years. Worked as a ranch hand and cowboy, moving cattle and supplies around the northern territories and to the goldfields of Montana. I wanted to see the world, but decided it was time to get home and check on the folks. I sent a few letters but never heard back."

"Ain't ye slightly heading in the wrong direction?"

"Nope. Got home about three weeks back to find the ranch burnt out. Cattle gone, and two unmarked graves."

"I am truly sorry, lad," Angus said as he poked the fire with a twig.

"At least whoever found them had the decency to bury them." Been searching and asking questions to anyone I run into on the trail."

"Sure, wish I could help ye out, kid. I reckon I've only been up in this neck of the woods fer about a year now."

"From what I could tell, the looks of things and the plant growth, it's probably been more than a year since it

to breed them. Over the last three years, they've had eight pups. Pops sold them all."

Jacob drove the runabout up to the barn, following Alisa's instructions. He secured the leather strap over the handle, locked the wheel brake, and quickly stepped around the buggy to help Alisa off. She stumbled into his arms and paused momentarily, looking up at him and feeling comfortable in his embrace. A bit embarrassed, she stepped back and brushed down her skirt. "Thank you, Mr. Long," she said somewhat shyly.

"You're welcome, Ms. McDuncan." "If we're back to using surnames," he said.

"Yes, you're right. I'm sorry. Thank you, Jacob," she said, smiling.

"You're always welcome, Alisa," he smiled back.

"I'll go find Henry. He takes care of the ranch area. Cali must be around since Barron is here."

"Great, I'll start moving some of these supplies into the barn. Tell Henry I'll give him a hand, and you can rest. It's probably been a rough day for you, and you could use it."

"I'm fine, thank you. I'm a lot tougher than you think."

Jacob smiled as he dropped the buggy's wooden gate. Yes, I can see that you are," he said, smiling at her. Then, he began moving smaller items around in the buggy's bed. "I'll come up to the house as soon as I'm finished helping Henry and introduce myself properly to your parents."

Alisa headed into the barn to find Henry.

Moments later, Alisa returned. "Henry's on his way out. I'll head in to let my parents know I've come home with a guest and freshen up a bit," she said, her voice light as she strolled toward the house. The sun cast a warm glow around her as she glanced back, her eyes catching sight of him. He was striding confidently, a large burlap bag slung over his shoulder. His hat was pulled low to shade his face from the sun, and he wore leather gloves to protect his hands, muscles flexing beneath his shirt as he balanced the weight of the bag. He was the perfect vision of a working cowboy. She smiled and hurried to the house.

Jacob knocked on the door, glanced down at the dog that had followed him from the barn. It sat beside Jacob, just staring with a curious, tilted head. "So, there are three of you? You know," he said, looking at the German Shepherd. I didn't get your name yet." The animal whined. "Not talking, are you?" But just as he was about to get an answer, the door opened.

The man standing before him was Alisa's father. His long, gray hair framed his face as he peered through a pair of spectacles. He wore Levi Strauss' "Waist Overalls," a white high-collared shirt, and a tan leather vest. His unshaven face, which he had neglected to trim for several days, added a rugged quality to his appearance. He stood as tall as Jacob, with broad shoulders and a proud, straight posture. Jacob immediately took a liking to him.

"You must be Jacob, then! Come in, lad!" he exclaimed, shaking Jacob's hand with a hearty grip before pulling him through the door and closing it behind them. "Come on, over here to the parlor. Take a seat, will ye? We'll get ye all settled in. There's a guest room upstairs, and Alisa's busy gettin' it ready for ye. Now, what'll it be? A wee dram of Scotch, perhaps? Ah, but hold on—I've got somethin' even better for ye: some fine Irish whiskey! Ye'll love this: it's Bushmills, straight from Northern Ireland," Rory said with a grin as he motioned for Jacob to sit down. He opened the whiskey cabinet and started to pour. "Ye see, this stuff's been around nearly 300 years, ken? Back in 1608, it was the very first distillery ever granted a license to produce and sell whisky in all o' Ireland!"

The large leather chairs they sat on were comfortable. They were placed on either end of a small round Georgian-style table, a few feet from the stone hearth fireplace. Above the fireplace, a gun rack holding two repeating rifles was mounted.

The conversation was brief, and the drink was even shorter. Alisa and her mother, Sophia, entered the room. "Gentlemen, I apologize for interrupting your discussion, but Alisa needs to show Mr. Long to his room and the washroom so he can prepare for dinner. "Mr. McDuncan, you should check in with Henry before you retire for the evening. I've taken supper out to the hired hands, so it's just us and our guest tonight," Sophia said.

"Yes, ma'am," Rory replied as he stood up. He grabbed his hat, thanked Jacob, and walked toward the door. Jacob only learned a few things from their visit: the history of Irish whiskey, that Rory was a twelfth-century king in Ireland whose name means "red king," and that the third dog's name was Shepard.

After washing up, Jacob properly introduced himself to Alisa's mother, Sophia, who promptly seated him across from Alisa just as Rory entered.

"Great, everyone's here. Let's say a wee prayer." They all joined hands. "Lord, bless this fine feast and help us to be grateful for yer mercies. Teach us to ken who feeds us and for the bounty of spuds we're blessed wi'. Bless us with Christ, the living bread."

Jacob put his napkin in his lap. "You must really be blessed with potatoes?"

"What? Oh, t' potatoes and t' prayer, yes, we are blessed. I give t' good Lord thanks every day we were here in America twenty years ago rather than in Ireland during t' potato famine tat wiped out t' potatoes. A million people starved, they say. The *Great Hunger* they called it, Aye. There's an old Irish blessin': *Be eatin' a potato, peelin' a potato, have two potatoes in ye hand, and an eye on two more on t' table.*"

"Enough talk now; plenty of time for talk later," Sophia said.

Jacob laughed, "Yes, ma'am. Okay by me. I'm hungry."

As she began to pass around the food, Alisa got up, went to the stove, took a large bone-in rib steak from the griddle, and dropped it on Jacob's plate.

Rory paused and stared up at Alisa, "What, you're not going to let the lad find his own heart's calling before he's even had a chance tae decide, are ye?"

"Now you hush," Sophia said. "You know darn well you're the only one who likes it at every meal. And what if he didn't like it?" she pointed at Jacob. "Would you want him to go hungry the first night of his visit? Why, he'd never want to come back. Now, is that what you want?" Rory fell silent.

Sophia looked at Jacob and said, "Colcannon is meant to be a side dish," pointing at Rory with her fork. But he thinks it's a main dish, so I add some pork sausage, or he'd never get any meat."

"I'd gladly share this steak with you, Mr. McDuncan, if you'd like; it's big enough for both of us."

"No, no. You enjoy it," Rory said while smiling. "I'm perfectly content wit' what I have, I am. But don't let this dish pass you by; you've got tae give it a go fer yourself, laddie."

"Yes, sir," he replied curiously as Rory handed him the large bowl. "If it has cabbage and sausage, I'll like it," he said, then scooped a generous spoonful onto his plate.

Jacob began eating his Irish dish before moving on to the steak. He smiled and winked at Alisa, who was already grinning from ear to ear.

Chapter Four

IT WAS THREE IN the morning when the triangle bell began to ring outside the house. Jacob woke, sat up in alarm, and grabbed the gun from his gun belt hanging on a chair next to his bed. When his senses came to him, he slightly opened the door and peeked through. He could hear a commotion coming from the main floor. Just then Alisa came up the stairs. Jacob stuck his head out the door. "What is it? What's going on?"

"We're under attack. They tried to burn down the barn, but Henry was able to stop them. The hay pile is on fire, and Henry was shot."

"I'll be down shortly," Jacob said, stepping back into his room. He looked out the window as he dressed and put on his gun belt. He was at the back of the house, and all the action seemed to be around the barn and corrals.

Jacob opened the window and peered outside. After confirming the coast was clear, he carefully stepped onto the roof of the back porch and descended to the ground. With his gun in hand, he crouched down and waited momentarily. The moon was bright, making it easier to see. He remembered a ravine a few yards off when he first rode in with Alisa.

He hurriedly made his way to the shallow ravine, descended into it, and carefully plotted a course through the rugged terrain away from the ranch. When he felt he was far enough away, he looked over the top. He could see the flashes from sporadic gunfire. Now that he was behind it all, he climbed out through a brush and tree-lined hillside. He was now behind the invaders.

Determining his next move wouldn't be as easy. It was difficult at night to tell how many there were. He could make out three locations of gunfire and decided to make his way to the closest. Crouched down, he quietly made his way to a tree nearest to the gunman. He waited a moment to make sure he wasn't heard, then stepped out with a gun in hand.

"Give it up, mister. You've been had." But as he spoke those words, the marauder turned and fired, but it was too late. The kid's bullet struck the attacker in the chest. He was dead before he hit the ground. Jacob quickly moved to the man and checked him. He was gone.

Taking the dead man's rifle, he checked it, then pulled some .44 ammo from the dead man's rifle sling and reloaded it, then slipped the sling over his head, hanging across his chest. Taking the 44-40 Winchester now gave him the advantage since his rifle was in the barn with his horse. He could make out three figures in the dark from his new position and started shooting.

One of the three went down and yelled out, "I'm hit. Someone's shooting from behind us. I need help. Get me on my horse."

From the banter, Jacob could tell the men were helping thier companion. He reloaded the rifle, then unloaded toward the attackers. When he was out of ammunition, the shooting had stopped. He could hear the horses' hoofs trailing off into the distance. He again, reloaded the rifle before he moved from his concealment. "Hold your fire," he shouted. "It's Jacob. Don't shoot; I'm coming in."

"Okay, but take it slow with yer hands up," a voice replied.

Jacob moved from his position but first walked around the perimeter of where the abusers were to make sure none had stayed behind, then raised his hands and rifle above his head and started in. "I'm coming in," he repeated.

Someone with a rifle trained on him was approaching. "Jacob, is that you?" It was Rory.

"Is everyone okay?"

"They are," he said as he drew closer, then stopped. "Henry's shot. Just a wound… Daft, man, what're ye doin' way out here?" Rory looked around for the ambushers his brow furrowed in confusion as he scanned the rugged landscape. "They're gone," Jacob remarked.

"Thought I heard horses in the distance."

"A couple of them lit a shuck on one horse. One didn't make it. I don't want to leave him out all night. I'll get the wagon, and we can bring him in. We don't want critters to disfigure him before we can see who he is and take him into town for the sheriff."

"Alright, but first we need t' attend tae t' hay fire so it disnae spread."

Rory and Jacob pulled up with the wagon. Rory climbed down and, taking the lantern hanging on the wagon, walked to the body where Jacob was already standing. He bent down to look at the man's face with the lantern light. "Aye, can't say I know him. Maybe a drifter."

"No, I know him, or of him. He's one of the two men who accosted your daughter in town."

Rory glanced up at Jacob with a bewildered look on his face. "Well, I'll be. He's gotta be working fer somebody. This couldn't be just a random incident – too well planned out." Rory looked down at the dead man, "Well, mate. I'd say ye got what was a coming to ya."

The morning came quickly. Jacob walked into the dining room. The women were still preparing in the kitchen, and Rory, Cali, and Henry sat at the table.

"Sorry, I overslept. Been a long time since I slept in a soft bed."

"No worries," Rory said. "Come, sit down."

Jacob pulled out a chair and sat down. "Good to see you're still kicking, Henry," he smiled.

"Ah, It was a flesh wound. Not very deep. Mrs. McDuncan is a master with a needle and thread."

"Still, glad to see you're okay."

Just then, the ladies walked out and sat down a pan of Johnny cakes and muffins. "We'll be right back with steaks and beans," Sophia said.

They did not discuss the dead man for the women's sake. The breakfast conversation was light, the men excused themselves and headed out to the barn.

"Since Henry's arm is out of commission," Rory began to instruct. "Cali, get the horses hitched to the wagon so we can head to town." Cali nodded his head and ran to the barn. "Henry, make sure the women have rifles in the house just to be safe. We'll be back near noon tomorrow. Listen to me. Don't leave t' ranch unless ye have to, and never go anywhere alone. I'd rather have ye here patrolin' than caught in an ambush. We good?"

"Yes, sir. We'll hold down the fort. Those women can shoot as well as any man," Henry said.

"Aye, can't argue wit' tat, or them for tat matter," Rory added with a chuckle.

A few hours later, the wagon rolled into town. It was early morning, and the town was coming alive. People were hurrying about, crossing the street, and the wooden sidewalk clamored as customers made their way in and out of the local shops. Jacob pulled the wagon up to the front of the sheriff's office, locking the wheel brake into place.

As the two men climbed down, Sheriff Thompson and Deputy Payne came out of the office, meeting the two on the boardwalk. "Morning, Rory," the sheriff said. "Who's your friend?"

"Sheriff, this is Jacob Long, a mate of my Alisa. He's staying with us fer a few days. Jacob, this here is Sheriff Douglas Thompson, and Deputy Leroy Payne." They shook hands and exchanged pleasantries.

"So, Rory, what can I do for you today?" Sheriff Thompson asked.

"Last night, we were set upon. They tried tae set the barn on fire, but Henry stopped 'em and saved the barn, so only t' hay pile went up in flames. He took a bullet in t' arm, but he'll be grand."

Rory walked around the wagon and gestured to follow. "This one didn't make it. Ye know t' fella?" he said as he pulled the burlap blanket away from his face.

"Isn't that one of the hard hands that works for Frank Wettin?" Deputy Payne asked.

"I knew it," Rory said in disgust.

"Hush, Payne," Sheriff Thompson said.

Jacob walked closer to the Sheriff with a suspicious look on his face. This is one of the men who attacked Ms. Alisa yesterday in the alley at the mercantile. He had another man with him. A big, burly fellow. They acted tough and threw threats as if it were common talk."

"That's right," Rory added. "Jacob saved my daughter from em two no-good coon dogs. Ye know Wettin's been trying tae push me and others out since he's got here. Wants all the good land for himself. Well, he ain't a gettin' it, no way, no sir. And now, he's tryin' tae kill us."

"I understand that you're upset about your daughter, and I'm sorry, but you can't just make accusations without evidence. We don't know why this young man attacked your daughter and your ranch. There's no proof that it was Wettin. And you, young man," looking at Jacob, "should have come to me if there was trouble in town. It's possible he was seeking revenge for what happened yesterday.

Baloney, Sheriff. Ye know darn well what's been going on. Why, t' whole town knows. It doesn't take long fer people to talk. And when em cowboys get liquored up, ye know they run their mouths off."

"Tell you what, Sheriff." Jacob butted in. "We'll drop him at the coroner's office. You can inform Wettin that one of his men was killed in an ambush on the McDuncan ranch, and he or you can do what you want with the body.

No one said another word. The sheriff was not helping. The body was dropped off at the coroner's office, and it was explained that the situation was now in the hands of the Sheriff.

"If you don't mind," Jacob said as Rory climbed onto the wagon, "I'd like to visit the General Store and Pawn?" He pointed to the sign a couple of buildings down. "I'd like to snoop around for a while."

I'll get us some rooms, then."

"Great. I'll meet you at the Corner Café in an hour for supper, and then we'll head over to the Bottomers Saloon for a quick drink—my treat. Monte has a good bourbon selection and a quiet spot where we can sit and talk away from the crowd and noise."

"Ye' had me at supper, laddie. I'm exhausted and hungry. It's been a long day and ride to town—and tat drink, I'm holding ye to it."

Jacob watched for a moment as Rory drove the wagon toward the hotel. He then turned and stepped up onto the boardwalk and through the door of the General Store and Pawn. He paused momentarily, taking in the array of used merchandise surrounding him. Sturdy bed frames stood sentinel beside a worn collection of pots and pans; their surfaces blackened from years of use. Shelves held camping supplies showing wear from adventure—campfire coffee pots, rusted lanterns, and bags of blankets that had seen countless nights under starry skies. Leather goods of every kind, while tack and saddles, meticulously crafted, echoed the labor of skilled hands. Scattered among these were whimsical trinkets, mementos that miners had clung to as reminders of their distant homes, each carrying a story of longing and solitude. Now sold for cash, these treasures reflected an earnest struggle to survive.

As Jacob wandered through the store, he couldn't help but reflect on the memories of others, each moment carrying a bittersweet nostalgia of his own. As he passed a glass counter filled with women's essentials, he felt a gentle ache, a cherished memory of his mother combing her hair in the mirror. Jacob stopped. There it was in front of him: the memory of his mother using that ivory comb to hold back her hair. She always said that no two were ever alike.

Chapter Five

THE NEXT DAY, JUST in time for lunch, Rory and Jacob arrived at the ranch. Alisa's eyes sparkled with enthusiasm as the food was passed around. She turned to Jacob and asked, "Would you like to ride with me into the hills? I want to show you around the ranch." Jacob felt a curiosity he couldn't quite place and quickly finished his lunch, unaware of the gleam in Rory and Sophia's eyes as they watched the two youngsters interact.

It was a perfect day. The hills were green and lush, with wildflowers blooming and songbirds singing. The creeks flowed with fresh water from the high mountain snow. Shade from the Arizona Ash trees kept the ride cool, while juniper and oak trees dotted the hillside among a forest of Ponderosa and Pinyon pine. They reached the crest of the hill and paused; the world spread out before them. Alisa spoke passionately, vividly illustrating the potential and value of the land. Jacob listened in silence, absorbing her words. She hoped that her descriptions would inspire him to stay, feeling as if the very essence of the land connected them. Deep down, she longed for him to remain, knowing she might never meet someone as remarkable as him again.

Jacob tipped up his hat and leaned forward against his saddle horn. "The beauty of the mountains and land doesn't compare to the lady riding beside me," he said. Lowering her head, Alisa blushed. "Any man would be a fool to want to leave all this."

Jacob dismounted his horse and extended his hand to Alisa, guiding her down with a gentle touch. As they stood together, a physical warmth enveloped them, Jacob's arms wrapped around her in an embrace that felt protective and intimate.

"If I had encountered you here under different circumstances, nothing—not even wild animals—could have pulled me away. Right now, my mission is to find the outlaws who murdered my parents and burned down their ranch," Jacob paused. "I have a lead, and I've got to act on it."

Alisa slightly pushed away. "A lead? What kind of lead?"

Jacob walked over to the saddlebag on his horse and took out the comb. "This," he said as he handed it to Alisa. "I found it at the General Store. It belonged to my mother."

"It's beautiful, Jacob," she said as she examined it.

"When I was young, I would watch her put it in her hair. She always told me it was one of a kind. See the detail inlaid into the Ivory?" I remember them as clearly as day." He pointed them out. "I told the storekeeper what had happened and offered the full price if he would share any details about the man who sold it to him.

"Does my father know?" She carefully handed the comb back.

"He does. We had a long discussion about what I should do. He understands." Jacob neglected to mention that half the discussion was about her. "I need to find them and bring them to justice one way or the other. I hope you can understand."

"I'll do my best," she replied. "It'll be challenging, but I'm willing to try. From the moment I saw you, I knew you were different. I don't think any other man in the territory would have done what you did for me. I feel truly blessed and grateful that you came into my life when you did. I will never forget this.

The couple started walking, their horses in tow. "Many men have courted me, but I've never felt drawn to any of them until I met you. I apologize if I'm being too forward. It's just that my father always said, 'Never look a gift horse in the mouth, and never let a good thing pass you by.'"

Jacob smiled and took her hand. "I have to admit, I was captivated by you the moment we met. The way you stood up to those ruffians was more impressive than anything I experienced with any woman during my travels."

They stopped and faced each other. "I have only one, maybe two requests," Alisa said. "First, that you stay as long as you can. I feel safe when you're around, and when you decide to leave, send me a telegram at least once a month. Even if it just says, 'I'm still kicking.' I'll be here waiting for you."

Jacob agreed, "I guess we should be getting back."

"Yes, we should. I have chores, and Pa will surely have made plans for you."

In no hurry, they continued their walk, enjoying the peaceful scenery and the warm sun on their skin. They were deep in conversation about Jacob's plans to locate the men responsible for his parents' deaths. Alisa's mind, however, was clouded with dreams of the future when Jacob suddenly noticed a pair of riders in the distance. As they approached, it became clear that the riders were two strangers, and Jacob couldn't shake the feeling that something was off about them. Jacob loosened his gun and stood slightly in front of Alisa as the two men rode up.

Both men were heavily armed. One man wore a bandoleer slung proudly across his broad shoulders, displaying a weathered ruggedness. He appeared to be part Indian, with striking features that hinted at his mixed heritage. His leather clothing was adorned with intricate tassels and beads that danced with the movement of his horse, each bead held a story of his life's journey. A flat-brimmed hat crowned his head, decorated with a single eagle feather. His whiskerless face revealed strong cheekbones and a determined gaze, suggesting lineage tied to the Comanche people.

Beside him stood another figure, gaunt, weathered, and unshaven as if a tall Ocotillo cast its shadow across his face. His hat was a battered relic, worn and frayed, much like his frayed clothes that hung loosely on his frame. A cross-draw holster clung to his side, housing a Colt .45 that glimmered ominously under the daylight. Despite his smaller stature, a raw, menacing energy radiated from him, making him seem the more dangerous of the two as if he'd seen and survived countless battles that had left their mark on his soul.

"Good day," Jacob said.

"Well, howdy to you and that fine-looking woman you have there," the skinny man said. Alisa stepped back behind Jacob a little more. "I'm Jacob. Are you heading to the mines for work or just passin' through?"

"Doesn't she have a name?" He gestured to Alisa with his head as he leaned on his pommel horn and smiled, displaying his dirty, jagged teeth.

"Her name is of no consequence. How about you fellas, got names?"

The mousy cowboy looked over at his riding partner. "Did ya hear that, pardner? She's a big word of no consequence." Turning back to Jacob, he said, "We're surveyors for the mining district. Just running some surveys.

Jacob studied them for a moment. "For surveyors, I don't see any equipment."

"Well now, we done left that back in the dust some time ago. Reckon we'll swing back 'round for it once we've wrapped up this ride of ours. Just wanted to soak in this lovely spot ya got here, darlin'." Jacob noticed. The man couldn't keep his eyes off Alisa.

Jacob's suspicions were confirmed when the strangers introduced themselves as surveyors for the pioneer mining district, claiming they were checking property boundaries. True professional surveyors would have been more respectful and polite.

Alisa stepped out from behind Jacob. "My father had never mentioned anything about surveyors, and it's highly unlikely for anyone to be surveying our land without his knowledge. The suspected gunman exchanged a quick glance with Alisa. The expression on his face changed.

Jacob stepped in without missing a beat. "Do you two surveyors have any credentials?" They dismissed his request and continued with their lie, pointing into the distance to try to draw Jacob's attention away. Jacob's instincts kicked in as they slowly moved their hands toward their guns, and he realized something was amiss. He could sense danger lurking in the air.

The gunman suddenly became hostile, changing their tone as they moved their hands over their guns. "Mister, I don't reckon I know you or this here woman you're fussin' over, nor do I care a whit about who you claim to be," the gunman screeched out. "You're a long way from civilization, and I couldn't give two plug nickels what happens to you out here in these wilds. Soon enough, this will be our boss's land and trespassers will be shot on site."

Jacob could feel his blood boil at their audacity. This was Alisa's family's land, and he wouldn't let anyone take it away from her.

Before the situation escalated any further, Jacob drew his gun with lightning speed. Alisa gasp. Jacob knew he had to keep her safe. He tried to reason with the strangers, but they wouldn't listen. It was clear that they were hired guns, and their only goal was to take over the land and kick the McDuncan family out, or worse.

The two gunmen, in shock, moved their hands away from their guns. "Gentlemen, I've been reasonable. But you've been burning your candle at both ends. You've lied, verbally molested my friend, insulted us, and threatened us. I'm done dealing with a couple of Razor Grinders. You either high-tail it back the way you came or find yourself admiring the beauty of these here hills under a dirt blanket. Which way will it be?"

The weaselly gunman spat on the ground. "This isn't over, mister."

"No, it is not, and I guarantee you this. Next time our visit will be much shorter. Now git!" The two gunmen turned and spurred their horses into a run.

Jacob grabbed Alisa and swiftly swung her onto her horse. He climbed onto his horse and spurred it into gallop with Alisa beside him. He wanted to get as far away as possible if the strangers were in pursuit. Jacob kept watch on his back trail until they reached the safety of the McDuncan Ranch.

When they were safely back at the ranch, Jacob explained everything to Alisa's father, who was shocked and grateful that his daughter was safe. Rory wanted to ride out after the men to confront them and get them off his land.

"Rory, I'm sure they're already out of the country. They didn't expect to run into us. Given the situation, we should be more cautious while riding and stay more aware of our surroundings. This is still untamed territory, and we shouldn't let our guard down."

"Aye, I suppose ye're right, Lad. Nae sense in forcing a shootout when we've got our women folk to look oot for."

Jacob patted Rory on the back as they headed out of the barn. "That, sir, is the best reason of all."

At the dinner table, they passed the plates while conversing about the day's activities. Sophia was worried, but Rory and Alisa convinced her it was an isolated incident.

Jacob didn't say much at dinner; he began feeling restless. It had been more than a week at the McDuncan Ranch. The longer he strayed from the trail, the farther the outlaws would get. During breakfast, Jacob confidently stated, "I need to take care of some business in town. If you need any supplies, put together a list. I'll take the wagon and pick them up while I'm there."

Rory put down his utensils and thought for a moment. "D'ye know, that's no' a bad idea at all. Henry did request some tack supplies earlier. Sophia, if ye need anythin', put a list together, lass. I'll double check with Henry as well."

Chapter Six

Jacob pulled the wagon up next to the side door of the mercantile building, the exact spot where he had rescued Alisa over a week earlier.

Jacob stepped onto the boardwalk and entered the front of the mercantile building; a bell rang over the door. The store resembled a quaint small-town mercantile, filled with a warm, inviting atmosphere. Rows of wooden shelving overflowed with an array of canned goods. On the floor, flour, beans, and oatmeal bags were piled in the corner, with some leaning casually against the walls as if they had just been delivered. Along the side wall were glass display counters, where mason jars showcased a vibrant selection of locally canned fruits and vegetables. In addition, jars filled with candies of every shape and hue were displayed on top of the counters, promising a delightful treat for anyone who ventured inside. This charming rustic atmosphere created a strong sense of community and nostalgia throughout the store.

"Can I help you, mister?" the store clerk said, startling Jacob from his sugary candy coma.

"Oh, yes, I apologize. I got distracted by your incredible selection of candies."

"Thank you. The miners spend as much on sweets as they do on tobacco."

"So, what can I help ya with?"

"Yes, of course. I have a list of supplies. This will be charged to the McDuncan Ranch. Rory said you would recognize it," handing the list to the clerk..

"Yes, I do. The supplies are consistent every time. Does Mr. McDuncan employ you?"

"No, I'm just a guest, a friend of Alisa. That said, I do my part to help out around the ranch. I also have a list of supplies I need. I'll be pulling out soon and paying for those myself."

"Not a problem. I'll get right on it."

"How long to put it all together?"

"Give me an hour, and I'll have it ready for ya."

"Great, I parked the wagon in the alley by the service door. I'll swing by and load it in an hour. Do you mind if I use your service door? I want to water the horses before I head for the saloon."

"Yes, anytime, and there's a bucket in the water trough."

"Thank you," Jacob said politely as he exited through the service door.

Making his way to the back of the building, he grabbed a bucket and leaned over to fill it. Suddenly, a sharp pain struck his head, and everything went dark.

When Jacob regained consciousness, he found himself in a bed. He reached up to feel the pain and discovered a bandage wrapped around his head. "Don't try to remove it," a voice said. "You need to keep it on for a while to prevent the stitches from opening and bleeding. I'm Dr. Allen Wright—doctor, dentist, and veterinarian in these parts."

"How long have I been out?" Jacob slurred.

"Three hours here and however long you were in the wagon."

"Wagon? I don't remember."

"What do you recall? Do you remember who hit you or what they hit you with?"

"I remember ordering supplies. Are the wagon and horses okay?" Jacob tried to sit up but was so dazed that he lay back down.

Don't try to get up just yet. Rest awhile. Let your senses return. Your wagon and horses are at the stable and well taken care of. When you didn't come back for your merchandise, the store clerk, Robert, went outside to check on your wagon, but it was gone. He sent his son to try to locate you and the wagon. As he began asking around, someone mentioned seeing a wagon and a team of horses near the creek on the northeast edge of town, but no one was around. That's where he found you and brought you straight to me."

"Thanks, Doc. What do I owe you?"

"Don't worry. I was informed that you're at the Mc-Duncan Ranch. It will be charged to his account. He looks after his own. Now, get some rest."

Jacob woke up early the next day. His head hurt less, but he still felt stiff, and his whole body ached. He slowly sat on the edge of the cot, waiting for the haze to clear. When he finally looked around the room, he noticed his gun belt hanging over the back edge of a chair and his hat on the other side. On the chair's seat, his clothing lay neatly folded, freshly washed, and pressed.

By the time he finished dressing, he was feeling better. Not long after, a young nursemaid knocked and then peeked in. "Oh, I'm sorry, sir. I brought some clean towels so you can wash up."

"Thank you, you can come in, I'm dressed."

The nursemaid, a young, long-haired Scottish redhead with a cute yet understandable accent, squeezed through the partially open door. "I'll just lay them here by the washbowl, aye. Is there anything else I can do for ye, sir?" She stood at the edge of the open door for a long time.

"No, thank you. You've been very helpful."

"Aye, but if ye need anythin', I'll just be here, I mean here, in the other room near here, sir." With that, she nodded and squeezed back through the door, closing it behind her.

After cleaning up some, he stepped out onto the main floor of the office. With the aid of his nurse, Dr. Wright was wrapping the arm of a miner who had injured himself. Looking up as Jacob came out of the room. "You're looking better. How are you feeling?"

"Much better. Thank you," he said before exiting the doctor's office. "You and your wonderful nurse have taken good care of me." The nursemaid turned slightly red and smiled.

"Thank you," the doctor replied. I'm glad to know that someone appreciates it," he said, looking at the miner unappreciatively.

Jacob squinted against the harsh glare of the morning sun, shielding his eyes momentarily as he grasped the railing of the worn wooden stairs, allowing his eyes to acclimate to the brightness. Once his vision adjusted, he slowly walked towards the stables, a familiar place filled with horses' soft neighing and the earthy scent of hay.

"Do you have the McDuncan Ranch horses and wagon stabled here, young man?" Jacob addressed the livery hand.

"Mister, are you alright?"

Jacob touched the bandage around his head, "Yes, I'll be fine….do you have the wagon here?"

"Yes, yes, sir, I do. And don't ya worry, none, the boss told me there's no charge to you. The horses are watered and fed. I'll get them harnessed fer ya right away," and the young man ran off to the stables behind the barn. Jacob sat down on a bale of hay and waited.

Thirty minutes later, the wagon pulled up in front of the livery. The stable boy set the brake and jumped down from the seat. "You're set."

Jacob got up from his hay bale and walked up to the wagon.

"All yer supplies from the mercantile are still in the wagon. It stayed with me in the barn out back where I sleep. Since it was with me, the boss had me tighten all the bolts, replace the worn brake rope, and grease the hubs and the springs," he said, rocking the wagon back and forth, quite proud of himself. "See, hardly a sound… Yes sir, should have a quiet ride back."

Jacob reached into his pocket for a coin, surprised to find one. Then he realized his leather bill wallet was still in his rear pocket. He was thankful the doctor and nursemaid were honest, then handed the young man a silver dollar.

"A silver dollar! Fer me? Thank ya, mister. That's two days' wages. Thanks a lot!"

"Well, after all your work, you deserve it." Jacob climbed onto the wagon seat, shook the reins, and rode out of town.

It was a long three-hour ride back to the ranch. Although he took a couple of breaks, sitting on the wooden seat, even with a cushion, it hurt like the dickens, as his pa would often say.

Jacob thought, *I might be sore and stiff* as he approached the ranch. *But, by golly, it was a mighty quiet ride!*

Jacob pulled the wagon up to the barn entrance. It was just past noon, and he was hungry. While unloading supplies, Rory walked into the barn carrying a rifle.

"Oh, my, lad. Looks like they got to ye too. It was a few days. We all was worried about ye, we were."

"Yes, I'm sorry. They gave me a good beating. Spent most of two days on the doctor's cot. Is everyone here all right?"

"Well, no, son, t's not." Jacob noticed the concern on his face, or was it fear? "Alisa couldn't handle the worry and headed to town with Cali."

Cali worked for the McDuncan family for three years. A trusted hand and a handsome young man with dark, slick hair, usually kept under a wide-brimmed sombrero. He had a clean face and a friendly smile. He embraced a Mexican style, featuring conchos on his saddle and tack, and adorned his harnesses with silver tassels and chamois skins. His appearance was that of a Charro. His name, Calico, was inspired by the wild horses of the Calico Mountains in Nevada. These horses are likely descendants of Spanish Barbs, and like these Spanish equines, Cali could quickly adapt to various environments and terrains.

"But they didn't make it." Rory continued, "They were ambushed. Thy' beat Cali something awful but wanted him alive to make it back here to tell me."

"What did he tell you?"

"Tat' if'n I don't run ye off, laddie, and deed t' land over tae them… they'll kill Alisa." From fear and worry,

Rory's Irish accent was so strong that Jacob could barely understand him.

Jacob felt exhausted, and his head ached. He didn't understand the urgency in Rory's words. He leaned against a post, taking a moment to gather his thoughts. "Ok, let me finish with the supplies, and I'll be in soon."

When Jacob entered the dining room, Rory and Sophia were both seated. As soon as he arrived, Sophia got up. "Oh, heavens! Rory told me you were hurt. You must be hungry. I'll fix you something to eat while you two men talk, then you should go to bed and rest. There's nothing we can do about anything tonight."

The two men sat in silence for a long moment. "I'll check with Cali tomorrow," Jacob said, "see if he's well enough to show me where they were ambushed. Maybe I can pick up their trail."

"I'll ride out with you," Rory added.

"If you don't mind, I'd prefer to have you here. You'll be two men short, and I'm not sure Henry alone can keep Sophia safe with his arm still bandaged. You might need to look after both of them." Rory looked at Jacob with a defeated look. "If I find a trail to follow, I'll send Cali back. It's safer to have more people here to keep the ranch secure. He can fill you in on my plans. If we don't find anything, we'll both head back and discuss a new strategy, agreed?" Rory shook his head in agreement as Sophia brought in something to eat.

At the table, Rory sat in thought while Jacob ate. "While you're gone," he said, "we'll fortify t' ranch so's we don't get caught by surprise again." Jacob nodded his head as he ate. "Finish chow, then head straight fer bed. I'm going to the kitchen to comfort t' Mrs. Don't get up in tae mornin' 'til yer ready—tomorrow could be a long trail.

Chapter Seven

WHEN JACOB WALKED INTO the dining room, it was nearly noon. Everyone had slept late, like he had, or hadn't slept at all, and the table was still set for breakfast.

"Henry and Cali have already had their breakfast, so they have!" Rory said. "They're bringing t' horses in tae get 'em saddled. Sit; I'll have t' Mrs. heat yur breakfast."

When Jacob finished breakfast, he headed for the barn, where the horses were tied to the fence. Cali walked out to meet him. "They are all ready to go, *señor*. Henry watered and fed them. He checked their shoes. All good to go."

"*Gracias*, Cali. How ya feeling? Up for the ride?"

"*Sí, señor*. No broken bones. I can ride."

"Glad you're still with us. Would you find me an extra canteen of water? I'm going to pack my overnight supplies. I don't know how long I'll be gone if we find their trail."

"*Sí, señor.* Mr. McDuncan put a looking glass in the barn to see, *lejos...* far away for you."

"*Gracias*, that'll be useful."

The two riders were less than a mile from the main road to town when Cali stopped near a rocky outcrop of boulders. "There, sir. Four *gringos* came out in front and behind us when we got there," he pointed to the middle. "*Señorita* Alisa was not happy when they hit me. She cried."

Jacob stepped down and walked over to where they had been ambushed. On one knee, he knelt to examine the markings on the ground. "Did you see what direction they went?" he asked, looking up at Cali."

No, *señor.* They didn't leave until I was *larga distancia* from here."

Jacob stood and began to circle the area. "Did you see anything else? Did they have any markings, clothing, or brands you'd recognize?"

I don't go to town much, sir. Don't see many people. Never seen them before.

"Tell me what you do remember."

They were *gringo* cowboys. *Cuatro de ellas...*" he held up his fingers, "four of them, sir, with *mascarillas* on their faces. One had a long beard and was *grande.* There was a brand on one horse; like *dos*, two," he held up two fingers, "horseshoes tied together... *acostados de lado.*"

"You mean they're connected together, lying on their side?" Jacob made two circles with his forefingers and thumbs and connected the two. "Like this?" he said, holding his fingers up for Cali to see.

"*Sí, señor.*"

Jacob circled the area. After a short time, he stopped, looked back down at the road and pointed. "Two of them headed for the main road, and the others went south into the hills. They probably kept off he main road to avoid being seen. Head back to the ranch, Cali. Tell Mr. McDuncan I'll follow the trail going south as far as possible. If I don't find them, I'll ride into town. Maybe I can find the horse." Jacob climbed back onto his horse. "And, if I'm not back by nightfall the day after tomorrow, tell him to find the sheriff and explain what happened."

"*Sí, señor.*" Cali began to turn his horse, then stopped. "Se*ñor,* I remember now. A man, his *sombrero* was, how you say *viejo.*

"You mean an old hat, in rough condition?"

"*Sí, señor.* And a vest, Mexican, *chaleco de color,* many colors vest, sir."

"Thanks, Cali, that will be very helpful." Cali nodded and headed back to the ranch.

Jacob headed into the hills, cautiously tracing the ambusher's path that twisted and turned through dense brush and thorny prickly pear cacti. The dry, cracked earth of the Arizona mountain foothills was dusted with sand, making the trail easy to spot. Sunlight filtered through the heavy vegetation, casting dappled shadows on the ground.

He was determined to press on, carefully maneuvering around the towering Saguaro cactus, its arms reaching skyward like a sentinel of the desert. The trail ended at a rocky hill. He climbed the hill and dismounted from his horse. As he reached the hilltop, the panoramic unfolded revealing itself, showcasing a breathtaking, vast expanse of rugged terrain. Jagged rock formations protruded from the earth, and the undulating landscape stretched far into the distance, dotted with desert flora. The sun cast a warm glow over the scene, illuminating the rich hues of ochre and rust that painted the distant mountains. He had lost their trail.

As Jacob rode into Pinal City, night had already fallen. It was too late to visit the sheriff or examine the branding on the horses. Exhausted from his journey and knowing he had a busy day ahead, he hitched his horse in front of the hotel, pulled his saddlebags, and booked a room for the night. At first light, he'd take his horse to the livery for feed and water while he looked around.

Jacobs's horse was pleased to see him. He was feeling hungry. When he dismounted at the livery, the sun had just peeked over the horizon.

"Well, look who's back," the young stable boy said as he greeted them. Jacob's horse neighed and lifted its head.

"Well, he's clearly happy to see you—he must know he'll get fed and watered."

"Yes, sir. I'll take good care of him. How long you staying?"

"Probably pull out just after lunch."

"Good, good. He looks a bit trail-worn. He'll have time for a bath and rub down.

"And, what do you charge?

"Boss wants half a dollar for full care or two bits for just boarding. But I'll take good care of him, sir."

"I'll take it, and there's something extra for you if you provide some information." The young man's eyes widened. "I'm looking for a rider with a branded horse—two horseshoes interlocked and lying on their sides." Another is a man with a colored Mexican style vest and an old worn hat. If you see anything, keep it to yourself and let me know. I'm Jacob Long. You should find me at the Grand Hotel or the corner café. I'll be there for breakfast and lunch," he said, flipping the stable boy a silver dollar.

"Yes, sir. Not a word." The young man then led the horse into the stable.

Jacob headed back up Main Street. Nearly twenty horses and mules were tied up along the main street at various locations. Several saloons remained open around the clock, creating a haven for heavy drinkers who poured most of their earnings into endless rounds of drinks. They could not afford a hotel room or pay to stable their horses with their funds depleted. So, they lingered in the dimly lit saloon throughout the night, surrounded by the murmur of conversations, the clinking of glasses, and the occasional snoring.

Jacob decided to walk down the opposite side of the street from the sheriff's office. By the time he circled back, the sheriff might be there. He began to walk slowly and quietly behind the horses lined up along the street. He didn't want to startle them, and if he needed to get closer, he would softly talk to them before touching them to get a better look at the brand.

Jacob had almost reached the end of the street when a miner, still drunk and clutching a drink, staggered out of a small shack that housed a saloon. As the miner stepped off the boardwalk to turn the corner and relieve himself, he noticed Jacob hiding behind a horse. "Hey," he called out. What the tar-nation are you doing behind that horse?"

Jacob raised both his hands and slowly walked toward the miner. "I'm sorry, mister," he said. "I'll explain it to you," he said as he came up next to him. "I lost something." Jacob placed his left hand over the top of the man's glass to avoid dropping it. "Here, let me hold this for you." The drunk looked down at Jacob's hand holding his glass, then looked back up. As he did, a powerful fist knocked him into a half circle, and he fell to the ground, Jacob still holding the whisky glass.

"I'm sorry I had to do that. I can't risk being found out." Jacob shook off the pain in his right hand while staring at the silent miner. "Mister, I'm sure glad you were drunk 'cause your face is as hard as a rock," he said, setting the glass down on the ground beside him before heading back to finish his search.

When Jacob reached the sheriff's office, he still hadn't found the branding he was looking for. He stood in front of the office. Its shades were pulled down, and the door was locked. "Must keep banker's hours," he muttered, then looked around. Believing the sheriff wouldn't show up soon, Jacob stepped off the boardwalk and headed across the dirt street to the café on the corner.

Deep in thought he watched as each step caused light dust to swirled around his boots. He looked up when he heard his name.

"Mr. Jacob, sir, Mr. Jacob, sir," came a voice from a distance.

The stable hand caught up to him, "A fella came in last night near midnight, he did. Woke me to rent him a stall. It was dark, but that colored vest he wore stands out.

"Nice job, thank you. And remember, tell no one of this. I'll be by after lunch to settle up my bill." The young man nodded his head and began his run back.

Jacob stepped onto the boardwalk and walked through the door of the corner café. "Good morning, sir. Please take a seat anywhere," the young lady said with a polite smile.

He was about to head for a table when he spotted a colorful Mexican vest at the back corner table. *Of course,* Jacob thought, *the outlaw's table; you sit with your back to the wall and can see who enters and everyone seated, and that's the table I wanted.* He noticed the man's meal was almost finished, so he chose a table by the window and sat down with his back to the Mexican vest. This way, when the man left the café, he could look out the window to see where he was going.

The polite young lady stood beside him. He hadn't noticed her. "Morning again," she said. "Today, we have steak, eggs, beans, and freshly baked muffins with cream butter, and I just made a fresh pot of coffee. What can I get ya'?"

As the young lady took Jacob's order, the man in the Mexican vest walked past and exited the cafe. Looking up at the young lady, he smiled. She turned red. "I'll have a little of everything and some coffee. I'm hungry, and the café smells good. So, I'm guessing the food is good too?"

"Yes, sir, that'd be the muffins," she said with a flirtatious smile and voice. And if you don't like it, I bet you'd eat it anyway." Jacob smiled again. "Yes, ma'am, I reckon you're right." She turned on her heel and headed into the kitchen. Jacob turned his gaze back to the window. He watched as the outlaw walked down the street and entered the Palace Saloon. Like any boom town, Pinal City had more saloons than any other business.

Jacob kept his eyes on the saloon. He'd finished his meal, and headed for the Palace Saloon. He pushed through the batwing doors, allowing his eyes to adjust to the dim light as he surveyed the room. He walked down to the end of the bar and took a seat. The bartender approached him, and he ordered a beer. The Mexican vest was playing Faro with other miners and drifters. An hour later, he heard the outlaw cuss. When Jacob looked over, he was digging around in his pockets. The Faro dealer said, "Sir, are you placing another bet?"

"No!" the outlaw replied. "Damn whore, got all my money."

Jacob thought, *That's why his horse wasn't at the livery until later that night. Must be a brothel somewhere on the edge of town.*

Jacob followed the man in the Mexican vest as he left the saloon and headed toward the stables. With no cash left, Jacob realized his only option was to return to the hideout where all the other outlaws were holding out. His dilemma was whether to confront the outlaw or try to follow him to the hideout. Following would be difficult. The sound of hoofbeats and the dust on the trail are clear signals to any rider that someone is tracking them. Nevertheless, he chose to follow.

Chapter Eight

Jacob cautiously followed the man to the livery stable, keeping his distance. Once the Mexican outlaw was inside, Jacob made his way around to the back of the stable to watch the outlaw saddle his horse and ride out. Jacob then rushed to the front of the livery barn to see which direction the outlaw was headed. As he did, he noticed the stable boy standing by the rear doors of the barn.

"I saw the man in the Mexican vest come in for his horse. Knowing you'd be watching, so I quickly saddled your horse. He's in great shape and eager to hit the trail."

Jacob took the reins and looked down at the horse's hooves, which were wrapped in shreds of burlap. "Ya sure are a smart lad."

"Figured you'd want to follow—keep the dust and hoof noise down."

He climbed onto the saddle. "Do I owe you any-thing?"

"No, sir. What you gave me earlier was more than enough." Jacob tipped his hat and rode out of the livery.

Riding approximately ten miles, Jacob followed the southern road that skirted the mountains, keeping his distance while tracking the path. It only took a few miles for him to recognize the distinct shape of the horse's shod shoes among others along the road when he came to a sudden stop. The tracks veered off onto a newly used trail. He paused in hesitation. Did the Mexican vest outlaw turn off because he felt he was being followed and was setting up an ambush, or was this the point he left the road for the gang's hideout?

Deciding to take a chance for Alisa, he drew his pistol and urged his horse into the thick brush to follow the trail. The animal's hooves softly tapped the ground as they followed the winding trail through the rocky foothills. The canvas-wrapped hooves kept the dust dispersed along the ground, allowing the rider to enjoy the rich scent of pine and wildflowers.

Holstering his Colt he pressed on surveying the rugged landscape. The outlaw's trail snaked toward the horizon, weaving through sunlit valleys and shadowy ravines. Despite the many secluded spots that offered perfect ambush opportunities, none had presented themselves, yet he remained on high alert.

He followed the trail east for about two miles, stopping under a large, blooming Joshua tree that shaded the path just before he climbed another hill. He didn't risk stopping at the top of the hill to give his adversary a recognizable silhouette. Whenever he crests a hill, he would peek over carefully before proceeding. After hours on the trail, both he and the horse needed a break. He climbed down and poured water from his extra waterskin into his hat for the horse and took a drink from his canteen. Looking around, he estimated that the McDuncan ranch was north or northwest of him, no more than four or five miles away. That's somewhat odd, he thought. Most of the cattle ranches are north of Hastings and Pinal City. Where was the outlaw leading him? He didn't remember Rory mentioning a ranch south of here besides the Mason Ranch. Most of them were closer to Florence. "It could be a hole-in-the-wall hideout in one of these deep ravines, like those in the Big Horn Mountains of Wyoming," he softly said to his horse.

He had ridden nearly four miles after their water break when he noticed his horse's ears perk up. At first, he hadn't heard it; it was the sound of pack mules with heavy hooves on the trail. Jacob veered off the trail and maneuvered around a large outcrop of stone. He quickly dismounted from his horse and peeked around the jagged rock wall. Four mules loaded with heavy packs came around the bend as he did. A man held the lead rope attached to the mules while another, armed with a bullwhip, ensured the mules stayed in line. Two outriders trailed behind, rifles in hand, as the mules obscured any signs of riders on the path. The outriders kept a vigilant watch on the horizon. Jacob leaned back against the rock. Curious about the pack mules. In this area, pack mules are primarily used to transport ore from a mine. Peeking around the large boulder he was convinced there were no others. Mounted his horse, he returned to the trail.

After riding for an hour, his horse slowly climbed a hill when he heard gunfire. Before reaching the top, he hobbled his horse. Although the horse was accustomed to gunfire, he didn't want it to start backing down the hill if it got spooked. He took a prone position at the summit. Three Apache warriors circled the man Jacob was tracking while one warrior lay dead on the ground. The outlaw concealed himself among a cluster of boulders. Jacob faced a dilemma. If he helped the man, how could he explain his actions, and would the man even provide the necessary information? If he chose not to help, the

Apache would likely kill him, leaving Jacob to continue his search for the hideout alone.

He didn't have to wait long. The outlaw stood and fired at an Indian on horseback advancing toward him; as he did, another shot an arrow into him, and he fell back to the ground. One of the remaining Apaches pulled out his knife and leaped off his horse, yelping a loud war cry. As he rushed at the outlaw, a bullet struck him, and he fell onto the pile of rocks. The last of the Apaches wheeled his horse around as if someone were behind him. He saw no one. The last thing he saw was the flash from the muzzle just as the bullet hit him.

Jacob quickly removed the hobble line from around the horse's legs and mounted. When he reached the boulders, he saw the man lying on the ground with an arrow sticking out of his chest. Jacob dismounted and checked to see if any Apaches were still alive before approaching the wounded outlaw. "Don't shoot, I'm not an Apache."

"Are you the one who helped me?" he asked in a gurgled tone, spitting up some blood.

"I am," Jacob said as he knelt beside the wounded outlaw.

"They kilt' me," the outlaw said as he leaned his head up to look at the arrow in his chest. He paused, then laid his head back down. "Thank you for saving my scalp."

"Mister, there's nothing I can do for you. I'm also glad they didn't take your scalp. But maybe you can do one good deed before you go. Help me out… for helping you keep your scalp and giving you a good burial."

The outlaw, in the blood-stained Mexican vest, tried to laugh but coughed. "Maybe—I can't remember the last time I did something good."

"My friend," Jacob said, trying to soothe the man and show he meant no harm, "I'm looking for the young lady your friends kidnapped a few days ago."

"Oh…," the outlaw moaned. "Mister, that was not my doing. I was paid to do what I was told… I didn't want to take the girl. I told them so, I needed the money."

"And you spent it all at the brothel."

"Ya, you were there?"

"It's no concern. What about the girl I'm looking for?"

The outlaw's speech slowed and became more diffi-cult to hear. "I didn't want to ride… with them back to the mine, so… I told them I needed to go to town."

"Mine? Is the mine their hideout?"

"It is."

"Who owns the mine?" The words were getting dif-ficult for the dying man to process. "Who owns the mine?" Jacob said louder.

"Don't know!" Then he coughed up more blood. "No one ever said… I never asked. Probably… not tell me anyhow," he said while coughing. Jacob knew he wouldn't last much longer.

"Where's the mine, and who's your boss?" The outlaw started to drift away. Jacob shook him and repeated the question. "Where is the mine? Who is your boss?

The outlaw regained consciousness and opened his eyes. "Curby. End of… trial," he slurred before closing his eyes for good.

Henry arrived at the house, banging on the door. Sophia hurried to the door and opened it. "Henry, what's going on?" she asked. Henry never banged on the door like that. Rory approached from behind her, joining her at the door. "Riders, coming in fast. Four of them. Cali's already at the corral."

"Alright. I'll grab my rifles." Rory hurriedly grabbed two rifles from the gun rack and a box of ammo. "Sophia, stay in the doorway for cover," he instructed as he handed her one of the rifles.

When Rory reached the corral, Henry and Cali were inside the fence with rifles ready. The road to the ranch curved around the large picket fence. Their position be-hind it provided good cover in a firefight. Rory arrived at the corner of the corral just as the four riders pulled up. "That'll be far enough," he hollered out.

The leader raised his hand, signaling for the men to stop. From afar, Rory recognized the lead rider and knew who he was. After the dust had cleared, Frank Wettin leaned on this saddle horn. "Nice weather we're having here, Rory," trying to sound casual and polite.

"Wettin, where's my daughter? And if'n ye lay a finger on her, I'll…"

Frank Wettin cut him off. "Don't you get your britches up in a knot. She's just fine. Some of my men are takin' good care of her. Now, have you done what I've asked?"

Rory raised his rifle. "I should shoot you right now and be done with ya."

"Now, you wouldn't want to do that. Then you'd never see your daughter again." Rory lowered his rifle. "Have you what I requested?"

"If'n yur' talking about the young man, I was told tae fire. He's moved on."

"Well, good. Then you're ready to sign the deed over to me. You'll get a fair price for your property. I've got the paperwork right here," He started reaching into his jacket pocket.

"Don't even pull that thin' out of yur pocket. I ain't sign'n anything 'til I get me daughter back."

Wettin removed his hand from his pocket. "Very well, then. Next time I see you, I'll have your daughter—and you'd better be ready to sign." Wettin and his hired gunmen turned and rode off.

Jacob buried the dead outlaw with the Mexican vest under a pile of rocks. He didn't have the time or tools to dig a grave. He wasn't worried about the Apache; they would likely arrive soon to retrieve their warriors. Jacob strapped the outlaw's rifle to his bedroll and placed the extra pistol, holster rig, and ammo in the saddlebags, along with the personal items he retrieved and one old letter. He knew the feeling of not knowing what might have happened to someone who headed west. He would send the letter and personal items to the address listed at his earliest convenience.

He mounted his horse, needing to find the outlaw's mine, assess the situation, and return to the ranch for help before sunup. A few miles later, he heard the sound of men at work, hammers striking stone. Spotting the cliffs in the distance, he turned southwest. He planned to work his way around the back of the cliffs to survey the area and hopefully locate the outlaw's mine and hideout.

After nearly an hour of navigating the rugged landscape, Jacob finally arrived at the majestic cliffs he had spotted from a distance. The air was dry and crisp as he dismounted, feeling the heat radiate from the ground beneath his boots; it had to be late in the day when temperatures were warmest. Carefully, he led his horse to a sprawling Palo Verde tree, its vibrant green bark contrasting beautifully against the golden desert hues. The resilient desert grass flourished in the refreshing shade of its leafy branches.

As Jacob approached the edge of the precipice, he surveyed the landscape. Shades of green, brown, orange, and copper dotted the view. Though rugged, it exhibited a unique beauty. Looking below, the area around the mine was wide open. Trees had been hauled in from a road leading in from the south. A horse and mule corral stood to the north, where the path he traveled ended or began. Nearby, there was a small log cabin with tents scattered around it. Jacob cautiously moved about ten yards south to gain a better view of the mine entrance, which provided him with a clearer perspective of the area. A few men with rifles, likely guards, were conversing with another man, presumably a miner. The mine wasn't very deep; they used picks and hammers to extract whatever they could. This explained why he could hear the sounds from the trail. Using dynamite would be too loud and potentially reveal their location.

He watched for nearly an hour, trying to get a good count of the men. Just as he was about to crawl back from the overhang, a man appeared, leading a woman to the outhouse. Moments later she came out and her guard followed her to the well. She filled a bucket and took it into the cabin. Jacob couldn't help but notice that she was remarkable, even in her rough state. Jacob thought, *Okay, she's in good condition and unharmed.* He needed to get back to the McDuncan Ranch and make plans.

The sun had just set by the time he reached the ranch yard. He stopped and waited, then called out, "Hello, the ranch."

A voice called back. "Who goes there?"

"It's Jacob."

"Come on in," said Henry. "We'd been waiting on ya."

He rode up to Henry, "Got news. Is Rory in?"

He's in the house—Cali's in the barn. He'll take yer horse."

"After removing his rifle and turning his horse over to Cali, he headed for the house. The door opened before he got there.

"Jacob, is that you?" a voice called out.

"It is," he said as he climbed the few steps to the porch.

Rory took hold of his shoulder. "Aye, Ya find my dear lassie, son?"

"Yes, sir, I did. She's doing just fine. However, there were too many of them; we need to talk."

"Aye, of course. First, you need food and some rest. I can tell yur plumb worn out.

Chapter Nine

FRANK WETTIN SAT BEHIND his office desk, rocking in his chair and brooding. He was not pleased that McDuncan was holding out on him in signing his deed over to him when a knock sounded at the door. "Who is it?" he yelled.

"It's Curby."

"Come in." Curby walked in and sat down in a large leather chair. "You find that young man, Alisa's friend?"

"I did not." He's either hiding or he's left the area."

"Well, don't count him out just yet. If he's privy to what's happening, he might not want to stay out of it. Keep your eyes open. I don't want him involved. Do whatever it takes to keep him out of it. Now, what about the girl?"

"She's fine, not causing much trouble."

"Good. I have important business matters to attend to in both Florence and Tucson. I need yo arrive at the territorial capital before they close to facilitate their move to Phoenix. I need Ms. McDuncan in good condition. She's my only bargaining chip to secure her father's ranch. If I fail to register these land deeds and mining claims by then, I'll have to travel to Phoenix. It could take months for the government to figure out what they're doing in the chaos. I can't risk the delay.

"How long will you be gone?"

"Three or four days at best. My meeting in Florence shouldn't take long and I'll leave for Tucson the next day. It shouldn't take no more than a few hours to get everything recorded in Tucson and I plan to head back that same day. Make sure that everything runs smoothly at the mine. While I'm away, the ranch foreman will be in charge here."

"Got it, boss. We should have enough silver ore by Thursday to ship a wagon to Florance."

"Great, and if there are any problems you need help with, let the sheriff know."

Curby got up and left the ranch without a word. Frank Wettin headed to his office to finish. He smiled as he tossed the deeds, he had coerced local ranchers into signing over to him and the registry for the illegal silver mine into his wall safe.

Sophia had put the final plate of eggs on as the men sat around the breakfast table. "Jacob, I don't quite understand. You said you only rode about ten miles south of Hastings?" Sophia asked.

"That's right, Ma'am. The other day, Alisa pointed out the hills south of the ranch. And you're saying that your land continues further?"

"Tats right," Rory added. "From the ranch, it'd be five miles. An' the Silver King Mining District expands a mile from my property line."

Jacob set his fork down, leaned back in his chair, and rubbed his chin. "Wettin's pullin' silver outta land that ain't his. So, not only are they digging into your land, they're mining illegally in the Silver King's district without authorization."

Tat's right, Jacob. If'n what ye say is true, we need to stop thos' thievin' coyotes.

"Should we tell the sheriff?" Jacob asked

Rory's grip tightened on his coffee mug. "The law doesn't care."

"Then maybe the Silver King Mining District will," Henry advised. "They don't like folks diggin' on claims that ain't theirs. First thing you need to do is ride to the Silver King Mine office and report what's going on."

"He's right, Rory," Jacob said. "Can you handle that?

"Aye, ye bet I can."

"Good. I want to ride into Pinal and see if I can convince the sheriff about what's been happening. Alisa was kidnapped to use as leverage in forcing you to sign over the deed to your land."

"Well, good luck with that, laddie. He's mostly a no-account varmint like those outlaws. Scared o' his own tail," Rory said in disgust.

"Well, I'll deal with it as I can."

"Sî, I'll get the *caballos* ready," Cali said as he headed out the door.

"You be careful riding to the mine," Henry told Rory. "You can't trust anyone. If'n, ye don't know em' keep riding."

Rory and Jacob rode into Hastings. Initially called Happy Hollow Camp, it later changed to Silver King Camp, then Queen before becoming Hastings. "Glad the Mrs. packed some snacks for us on this trip," Rory said when they stopped at the intersection that would take him to the Silver King Mine.

"That was mighty nice of her. When you're finished at the mine, head back to Pinal. If I'm there, I'll ride back to the ranch with you." Rory nodded his hat and rode north.

Jacob rode the rest of the way into town. His first stop was the sheriff's office. As he tied his horse to the hitching post next to the water trough, the sheriff emerged from his office with a stranger. The two shook hands, and Jacob overheard the sheriff say, "Sounds good, Curby. I'll take care of it."

Before the sheriff could reenter his office, Jacob called out, "Sheriff Thompson!" The sheriff stopped and turned around. "I remember you… Jacob Long, I believe. You brought the dead man in with Rory. I heard you had left town. Have you returned?" Jacob noticed that Curby had turned to look at him. He stepped onto the boardwalk and shook the sheriff's hand, wanting to be cordial. Curby walked around the side of the building.

"What can I do fer you?" the sheriff asked.

"I'd like to speak with you and Deputy Payne in private… if I may."

"He's not here right now. He should return in about thirty minutes. You don't want to talk to me; I'm free. We don't need to involve Leroy."

"No, I'm sorry. He'll need to hear the information I have as well. I'll go over to the café for a bit to get some coffee."

"Very well. Try one of their morning biscuits. They're pretty good."

Now the sheriff sounded cordial—*maybe a little too cordial,* Jacob thought as he walked to the café.

Curby stepped into the Bottomer's Saloon, looked around for a moment, then headed to a table in the back and sat across from his right-hand man. "Got a quick job for ya, Pike."

"Whatever it is, I can handle it," Pike replied.

"You still claiming to draw fast and shoot straight?"

"Faster and straighter than Bill Hickock."

"Ya, but he's dead. Shot in the back of the head by Jack McCall."

"Ya, I heard. They said he kilt 200 men… I don't believe it. Never did get a chance to challenge him, never in the same place at the same time."

"That skunk that kilt Little Billy at the McDuncan Ranch. Well, he's in town. The sheriff knows him. He called him Jacob Long."

"If'n he's here, I owe him twice now. I liked Little Billy. He had a mean, quiet deposition."

"That he did. What do you mean you owe him twice?"

"Little Billy and I had a disagreement with him a while back."

"Well, Pike, whatever beef you had, you have reason enough to put him under the dirt. I overheard him say he was heading for the café. Might be there a while. The deputy's not due back for a while."

When the barkeep, Monty, heard Jacob's name, he approached the outlaw's table to clear their empty glasses. The outlaws stopped talking when he approached. "Can

I get y'all another round while I'm here?" he said as he cleared the table.

"No, we don't need anything more; we're just about to head out," Curby said.

"No hurry," Pike said. "It's still early. I've time for another round," looking at Curby, hoping he would buy.

"Alright then, bring another round. Guess we're stayin' a while longer."

"Hey, Ricky," Monty yelled. "Get this table another round; I'll be in the back for a while working on the inventory," he said as he walked past Ricky, filling two mugs with beer. Monty walked into the back room and quietly slipped out the back door. He made his way along the rear of the buildings and across the street to the café, where he opened the back door and waved to the cook. "There's a young man in the café, a good-looking fella in a blue shirt. His name is Jacob. Please ask your girl to tell him to come here quietly; I have an important message for him." A couple of minutes later, Jacob stepped out of the back door.

"Monty, how are you? What can I do for you?"

"It's what I can do for you," Monty replied. "Two outlaws are in the saloon. I overheard them talking about you. From what I gathered, this fella named Curby is one of the ringleaders, and Pike is his demolition man, or at least that's what I've heard others call him--he's the biggest man around."

"I've heard of this Curby fella and I've had a run-in with this demolition man in the saloon. Busted up someone good."

"He was one of the two who accosted Ms. Alisa the day I arrived."

"You know, then, how dangerous they can be. Watch your back. Curby instructed Pike to take you out, and the sheriff knows. My guess.… he'll waylay you when yo leave the café.

"I would agree with you on that. I'll keep an eye open and pistol ready. Thanks for the information. I'll owe you another cigar and drink soon."

Monty smiled. "If'n that's how this works, I'm full of information."

"I bet you are," Jacob joked back.

"I'd best be getting back before I'm missed." The two men shook hands and parted ways.

When Monty emerged from the backroom with several bottles and a towel draped over his shoulders, both Curby and Pike had just finished their drinks.

Chapter Ten

JACOB FINISHED HIS COFFEE and returned to the café's kitchen, exiting through the back door. He looked around and made his way along the backside of the building, then continued along its side to the front corner. He scanned the street but saw no sign of the outlaws. After waiting a long time, he headed to the saloon. If the outlaws were still there, they could confront him then. If not, Monty might have more information.

He paused at the entrance to the saloon, taking a moment to look around at the street and the buildings. Nothing seemed out of the ordinary. As he turned to push through the bat-wing doors, something struck him square in the face, causing him to stumble backward, off the planked boardwalk, and land flat on his back on the dirt street. He shook his head to clear it. As he pushed himself onto his elbows, a large, burly figure came through the batwing doors—a bear. He shook his head again. No… not a bear. It was a man the size of a bear—a man he recognized.

"So, Jacob Long," said the bear-sized man. "I've been waitin' fer this day since ya ran me and Little Billy at gunpoint out of the alley by the mercantile. And now I learn you're the coyote that killed my friend. I'm gonna give you a beating before I put you under."

Jacob had just gotten to his feet. "You could at least tell me your name before you pummel me, so we've at least been properly introduced," he said with a bloody smile.

"My name's Pike," as he moved forward. "But it won't matter much in a few minutes 'cause you won't remember nothin'."

Jacob put up his hand in front of him to stop his assailant. He was stalling for time. "Come to think of it, the name Pike suits you. Don't you think?"

The big man got a confused look on his face. "How do you mean?"

"The name Pike, it's a northern fish, right?" the big man said nothing, just stared with a confused look. "Okay, you do have some qualities of a Northern Pike: it has a duck-like snout and sharp teeth. You do have sharp teeth, don't you?" The outlaw grinned, revealing his jagged and missing teeth. Jacob smiled back. "Well, I'd say that's a win."

Pike moved forward again, and Jacob raised his hand. "Wait, wait! There's one more thing you and the Northern Pike have in common… You ambush your prey." But just as Pike was about to smile again, Jacob unleashed a flurry of punches to his abdomen.

Pike stumbled back a couple of steps, his body instinctively bending from the force of the explosion that had rocked him. He caught his breath and looked up; enjoyment etched on his face. In an instant, before Jacob could grasp what was happening, Pike's powerful hands seized him, lifting him effortlessly off the ground. With a swift motion, he hurled Jacob, landing hard on the dirt street with a painful thud. The impact sent shockwaves through Jacob's body. After what seemed like minutes, he rolled onto his knees, grit and dust clinging to his skin as he gasped in agony. "Ow! That hurt," he said as he slowly stood.

Pike smiled and started after him again as Jacob extended his hand. "Okay, wait! I have another idea. I don't have a chance of beating you in a fair fight." Pike stopped to listen. "Why don't we finish this like gentlemen?"

"I don't understand."

"In the early days back east, when two men disagreed and wanted to settle it, the pistol was the item that made them equal. It would provide me with an equal opportunity in this dispute."

Piked laughed, "You still would not equal me. I'm faster than Wild Bill Hickock."

"Really? Did you ever go up against Wild Bill? I mean, if you had, you'd have killed him 'cause you're standing here with me."

Pike paused for a moment to think the question through. "No… I never had the chance. But I would have been faster," he said angrily.

"No, no. I believe you." Jacob said while holding up his hand again.

"I agree with you; you are probably faster. However, as a personal request, I would feel more equal in the fight with my Colt Peacemaker. They say that God created man, but Samuel Colt made them equal."

Pike chuckled. "Fine with me," pointing at Jacob. "You're still a dead man."

"Can you give me a moment to freshen up? I'm dusty and dry. Do you mind if I splash some water from the trough to cool off and clean the dust off?" Pike nodded, his fingers moving and stretching near his handgun. By this time, the crowd was growing.

Jacob walked over to the water trough, scanning his surroundings and the people on the boardwalks. He thought to himself, *Where's the sheriff in all this?* After splashing water on his face and hands, he dried his face with his sleeve and rubbed his hands on his shirt. He adjusted his holster, tightened his belt, and secured the tie-down on his leg before adjusting his Colt, ensuring it was not pushed in too tightly. Walking back over, he said, "I'm ready. I'll defer to your good judgment and decide how far away you want to be from me.

Pike didn't know what "defer" meant, but understood the sentence and began to back up. Like a signal, the crowd realized guns were about to blaze and bullets about to fly; they scattered like bugs.

Jacob moved his sore muscles and shoulders around to loosen them while waiting. Pike stopped and stood there without a word. "Again, I defer to you to draw when ready."

"Would ya stop saying that word? You're about to meet yur maker," he shouted while pulling his pistol. His deception didn't work. As the first slug hit him the jolt of the impact caused Pike's weapon to discharge into the ground, as two more bullets penetrated his body. Jacob had fanned the hammer three times to Pike's one.

Pike stood for a moment in shock, then dropped to his knees as Jacob walked up to him, reloading his Colt.

"That wasn't fair," Pike said while trying to stay upright.

"Sure it was. Colt made it fair. What wasn't fair is that I was faster than you." As he holstered his gun.

"How?" was all Pike could say.

"I had my gun worked on by a professional gunsmith in Denver. During my travels through Cheyenne, Wyoming, in '76, I learned a few things from Mr. James Butler Hickok. He was on a short honeymoon with his new wife, Agnes Thatcher Lake, before heading to the gold mines in Deadwood, South Dakota. He was bored, spending most of his time gambling, so I asked if he would give me some shooting tips. He gladly agreed. In confidence, he told me that his eyesight was getting bad and that he wouldn't shoot at any targets, but he still provided me with excellent instruction. He gave me the gunsmith's name to look up in Denver."

"Well, I'll be," Pike smiled. "You really knew Hickok?" Those were his last words as he dropped face-first into the dirt.

Just as Jacob holstered his Colt, he heard the sound of a hammer clicking back and felt the pressure of a gun barrel against his back. "You're under arrest, Mr. Long, for murder." Jacob lifted his hands.

Sheriff Thompson reached down and pulled Jacob's Colt revolver from its holster. Jacob turned around to face the sheriff.

"It was a fair fight, Sheriff, and Pike started it. I have witnesses to confirm that."

"I don't care what others say they saw. I know what I saw: You coerced Pike into a gunfight, and you'll hang for it."

Sheriff Thompson heard the sound of the hammer of a revolver clicking behind him." I'm afraid not, Sheriff." Deputy Leroy Payne had his gun on him. "Now, drop those guns, both of them!"

"You're making a big mistake, Payne. You're in over your head."

"No, sir, I'm afraid not. Everyone in town knows you're on the take and a hired gun for Wettin, including me."

"You've got no proof," the sheriff said in frustration.

"I do. Not only have many of the town's folks seen you talking to outlaws and Wettin, but I also recently overheard you talking to Curby. I was getting back early and came around the side of the building when I heard you through the open window talking to Curby, so I stopped to listen, and he informed you that if Jacob got in the way, you should kill him or arrest him on bogus charges. Just as you're doing now."

"You have no way to prove it," Sheriff Thompson spat angrily.

Jacob kept his mouth shut. He thought about adding that he had a witness who overheard Curby and Pike plotting to kill him, but decided against it. Right now, that would put Monty in danger.

"I don't need to," Deputy Payne replied. "By the time the circuit judge hears all the testimonies, you'll be basking in the warmth of the Yuma prison. One thing the judge can't stand is a crooked lawman. Now, put down the guns."

Sheriff Thompson slowly lowered his weapons, strategically turning and shifting his focus to Payne, determined to instill a sense of control. He wanted Payne to believe the tension had passed, allowing him to drop his guard just enough. As the tension seemed to dissipate in a calculated move, Thompson swiftly turned. In that split second, the air exploded with the thunderous sound of two guns firing simultaneously.

Jacob walked over to the deceased Sheriff Thompson, his eyes still open in shock. He picked up his Colt and holstered it. Looking at Deputy Payne, he asked, "Are you hurt?"

The deputy had holstered his weapon and was now holding his arm. "Just a deep graze. The Doc can stitch it up."

"He thought he had you," Jacob said, gazing down at Thompson.

"About did. If he had swung his arm or turned a little more, he might have hit me right in the chest, and we'd both be lying six feet under."

"Thanks for helping me. What made you think it was a fair fight? Jacob asked.

"I have never trusted him since I've known him," replied Payne. "I always kept my guard up with him while he hung around those outlaws. When I overheard his conversation with Curby, I decided to wait and see how he would react, although, I suspected he'd make the wrong choice. I'm sorry I didn't step in sooner. He could have kilt you. I was hoping not. He'd have to shoot ya in the back, but I suspected the crowd would have seen it otherwise; I'm sure he was aware of that.

"Well, either way, I'm glad you did, but it's not over yet. I'll grab a wagon from the livery if you can find some tough miners to help lift Pike. I'll take these two skunks to the coroner. Once you're patched up, we need to talk."

Chapter Eleven

CURBY QUICKLY SLIPPED INTO the shadows the moment Pike hit the ground. He'd never seen anyone fan the hammer on a six-shooter, nor had he realized it was possible. The air was thick with tension, and the gathered crowd was silent. Faced with the stark reality that he had no chance against Jacob in a showdown, he turned tail and ran.

Two hours later Curby was stood in the doorway to Wettin's office. "What do you mean he's dead? How could anyone beat Pike in a fight, either with fist or gun?" said Frank Wettin, owner of the Four Peaks Ranch.

"I'm tellin' ya straight up, after he realized he couldn't beat Pike in a fistfight, he talked him into a shootout. You know Pike fancied himself as havin' a faster draw than other gunslingers. I've never seen anythin' like it.

His gun was somehow modified. He fanned the hammer three times, and all his shots were dead on."

"What did Thompson do?"

"I don't know. I was afraid the crowd would turn on me. I didn't want to risk being involved, so I lit out. But I spoke to the sheriff earlier, and he said if'n anything went sideways, he would take care of it."

"Well, you'd better hope so for both our sakes. There's one thing I need you to do before I leave, and don't mess it up!"

When Rory rode into town later that day, he sensed something had happened. He couldn't quite put his finger on it. Perhaps it was the sound; the noise level seemed lower than usual. Small groups gathered together, but they spoke in hushed tones. The atmosphere felt dispirited. He rode up to the sheriff's office, dismounted from his appaloosa, and glanced around as he looped the reins around the hitching rail twice. As he approached the door, he lightly rapped on it to let whoever was inside know someone was coming in. When he opened the door and stepped in, Deputy Payne sat at the sheriff's desk. Sheriff Thompson didn't like anyone sitting at his desk. Rory's first response was, "Deputy Payne, where's the sheriff?"

"Mr. McDuncan, please come in. Jacob said you would be coming into town from the mine." Payne got up and pulled over a chair next to the desk. "Please have a seat. This might take a while to explain."

Jacob was headed back to the McDuncan Ranch. He and Deputy Payne had worked out a plan to get Alisa back. First, he needed some supplies, Cali, and an extra horse, to clean up after his fight and rest while waiting.

Rory McDuncan and Deputy Leroy Payne rode into the McDuncan Ranch around mid-morning. Rory had spent the night in Pinal City with Payne. Their main objective was to engage with the local townspeople about current events, inform them that Deputy Payne would assume the role of interim sheriff, and organize volunteers to ride out to the local ranches to announce that a town meeting would take place in two days at Bottomer's Saloon at half past noon.

Jacob and Cali came from the barn as Rory and Payne tied their horses to the corral fence. "How'd everything go in town?" Jacob asked.

"Better than expected," Payne replied. "Havin' Rory with me was helpful. His support as interim sheriff made a difference, and he's backing me in my campaign for the upcomin' election."

"Aye, the fact tat he stood up to Sheriff Thompson, who was in cahoots with Frank Wettin and his band o' outlaws, proved tae many tat he was a lad they could trust," Rory said.

"Congratulations, Sheriff Payne, if I dare say regarding the circumstances," Jacob said politely. I'm glad Rory stayed to support you. I think we have all the supplies packed that we need; Cali has Alisa's horse ready. We've got extra ammunition, blankets, ropes, and food for the night. Sophia is preparing an early lunch before we head out."

The four horsemen rode southwest, following the route Jacob had taken back from the outlaws' mine and hideout. They spoke very little during the journey; their minds were focused on Alisa and the plan. They aimed to arrive before sundown. The plan's first step was to set up a sheltered camp and create a separate area for the horses, far enough away to avoid being heard. After that, Jacob would show the men the mine and finalize their strategy following the survey.

After what felt like hours of trekking through the mountain foothills and canyons, the riders finally arrived near the mine. They discovered a suitable camping spot in a canyon beside a creek. There, they set up camp, watered the horses, and established a picket line in a grove of trees to keep the animals content.

"It's about two hours till sundown," Jacob said. "We're a good mile from the mine. We should have plenty of time to survey the area before we make our move."

Without conversation, the men gathered their supplies, rifles, and ammo and followed Jacob through the valley and up the backside of the mine. "Am I correct that this is your land, Rory?" Jacob quietly asked.

"It is indeed," he said, he said in his Irish brogue "It's been a bit of time since I've wandered out this way. I reckon me property marker is just another mile down the road, right near the end of the Pioneer Mining District, where it meets the Silver King Mine."

"Good, then we're within our rights to rescue Alisa and take the mine."

"Aye, it is," Rory replied.

The men reached the cliff's overhang above the mine entrance that Jacob had observed from days earlier. "There," he pointed. "The cabin is where they're holding Alisa. The tents near the cabin belong to the miners. I doubt they're gunmen, so be careful not to shoot unless they reveal themselves."

"How many outlaws did you see?" Sheriff Payne asked.

"We'll have to take our chances on the number of outlaws down there. When I was here, there were two outlaws or guards talking to a miner. I could hear voices and the sounds of work in the mine. I think it's still shallow, but with the number of tents, I'm only assuming there are four miners. Then, when I was about to leave, an outlaw brought Alisa to get water and use the privy."

"Rory looked at the men and said, "Or the Honey Pot as my women folk like to call it." All the men smiled.

"The trail comes in from the northwest, and to the south, there's a wagon road likely used to bring in the lumber laid out for the mine. If you've seen enough, let's head back down the hill to discuss the plan," Jacob said. The men settled into an arroyo surrounded by Desert Willow, Pinon Pine, and junipers.

Jacob began to explain his plan. "Rory, I need you on that ledge overlooking the mine, watching our backs. Sheriff, you and Cali work south down the canyon and wait. I will come in on the trail from the northeast. We'll wait until the miners come out for supper around the fire pit and take them by surprise. It'll be up to Rory to signal us with a rifle shot in the air when they gather for chow. Cali, it's up to you to cover the miners and keep them from finding a weapon. If they run for the mine, let them go. Odds are there's no weapons in the mine. So, hold them there at the entrance, *Comprende?*"

"Sí."

Sheriff Payne, there's a front and back door to the cabin. You distract them by hollering they're surrounded by a posse and to come out with their hands high. But keep back or find cover in case they decide to start shooting. As long as they're distracted toward you, I'll go through the cabin's back door and take them by surprise. Rory, to make it look and sound like they're surrounded. Fire some shots at the cabin, and no one shoots through the windows. We don't want to risk a bullet or ricochet hitting Alisa.

"Ya got it, lad," Rory said. "Jest get my gal safe."

"Unless there are questions," Jacob paused. "Okay then, let's head for camp, gather our horses, and head out.

An hour later, all were set in place for the raid on the mining camp. Rory was at the top of the ridge watching as four miners came out of the mine and headed for the cook fire. Two outlaws were there already preparing the meal. Rory waited until they were eating when a third man came out of the cabin, dished up two plates, and then headed back for the cabin. Not knowing how many were in the cabin, Rory had to make the decision to prevent the third outlaw from returning to the cabin—shoot now or wait. He took aim. This would be the signal. He fired, hitting the outlaw in the leg. The food and tin plates flew at the same time Cali and Payne came riding in and firing. They circled the cookfire. One of the two outlaws eating dropped his plate and went for his gun. Just as he drew, Payne shot him through. He dropped to the lap of his partner, who immediately raised his hand, hollering, "Don't shoot, don't shoot."

When the posse rode in shooting, the miners instantly dropped to the ground and covered their heads.

"This is Acting Sheriff Leroy Payne. You are surrounded by my posse. Come out now, and you won't be harmed!" He and Cali dismounted and knelt behind the fire while the others lay on the ground around them.

Moments later, the door opened, and rifle fire spat dirt and sand around them. "No lawman is taking me in," a man from the cabin called out. "I've got a hostage here with me. I will kill her if you don't saddle up."

Before the shooting started, Jacob, on foot, had already made it to the cabin. He had peeked through the rear window and watched an outlaw leave with two plates for grub. He checked the door as the man inside hollered at the posse. It was unlocked. Jacob burst through the door just as the man told them to saddle up. The outlaw turned to shoot at the intruder, but it was too late.

Payne and Cali watched as the man in the cabin turned in front of the door. A handgun fired twice, and the outlaw stumbled backward through the door, landing on the ground with a blank-eyed stare at the sky.

"Cali, cover the prisoners. I'm going inside," the sheriff instructed.

When Sheriff Payne entered the cabin, Jacob was sitting at the table with his pistol still in his hand. "She's not here," he said, looking up at Payne. "I don't know what to tell her father."

"We still got us one highwayman and four miners. I bet they'll spill the beans to save their hides." Jacob nodded, and the two left the cabin.

As the men walked to the campfire, Jacob seized the outlaw by the shirt and hoisted him onto one of the logs encircling the fire for seating. "Start talking," Jacob ordered. "Where's the girl?"

"I'm not telling you nothin', you kilt my friend."

Sheriff Payne interjected, "If you give us the information we need, I'll put in a good word for you to the judge. Maybe reduce it to an accessory to kidnapping."

"And what makes you think I'd tell some stinkin' coyote of a lawman anything?" the outlaw said, spitting on the sheriff's boots.

Jacob drew his Colt and smashed it into the outlaw's face, knocking him out and to the ground. Turning to Cali, he said, "Get those miners on their feet."

Cali helped some of the miners to their feet. Just then, Rory rode in at a gallop, swung down from his horse, and walked over to the cook fire.

"Alright, gentlemen," Jacob began. The same questions apply to you: Are you gonna cooperate or find yourselves in prison for kidnapping?"

"No, sir," said one of the miners. Directed their attention to Jacob and the man with the badge. "Sheriff, you've got to believe us; we had nothing to do with this. Those marauders took us hostage, too, and forced us to work this mine. We don't have any guns, clothes, or horses."

"What about the girl?" Payne asked.

Given the circumstances, Rory cast a doubtful glance at Sheriff Payne, realizing that Alisa was not in the camp.

"They came in at first daylight for the girl," the miner said.

"Who came for the girl?"

"The outlaw boss."

"You mean Wettin's outlaw leader, Curby?" Jacob asked.

"Yes, sir. That's what we've heard him called."

"How many were there? Did they say where they were headin'?"

"Counting Curby, there were six. All looked to be gunmen."

"And where were they headin'?" Rory chimed in.

The miner glanced at him, then at the other miners, shrugging his shoulders. One of the other miners spoke up. "They didn't talk much around us, and much of the time, we're in the mine. I came out for water; I only heard the word "ranch."

"Most likely, they moved her tae Wettin's Ranch. He's meant tae come by the ranch t' day after tomorrow with Alisa, so I can sign t' property deed over tae him, don't ya know?" Rory said.

Jacob sat down on one of the logs around the fire, his eyes dark. "He's got her. And he ain't lettin' her go 'till you sign," he said to Rory.

Henry let out a slow breath. "That's not good."

"That's right," Jacob muttered. "Wettin's the kind of man who couldn't care less about another person as long as he gets what he wants. If you sign, Rory, the ranch is gone. If he don't—" Jacob's jaw tightened." —she ain't got long."

"Over my dead body," Rory said.

Jacob met his gaze. "Not going to happen if I can help it—we must hit Wettin's ranch." Everyone fell silent and stared at the fire.

Rory looked over at the miners standing in silence and walked over. "Men, I own t' property this mine is on, and it's also within the Pioneer Mining District. I've talked with t' Silver King Mine operator, who's given me a letter of intent tae operate this here mine 'til I can legally register it." The miners listened with interest. "So, listen up, gentlemen. Ye have two paths ahead of ye. Ye can saddle up and ride outta here with these outlaws' horses, including those in t' corral, an' takin' any weapons and cash, these scoundrels have as yer pay, or if'n you're keen tae stick around and labor in this here mine, I'm a offerin' ye a forty-eight percent stake in t' mine. I'll only claim twenty percent of t' profits. If fortune favors us, ye could all be very wealthy men."

The miners exchanged excited glances before turning to Rory and enthusiastically shaking his hand. "We are honored that you would have us as partners, sir," one of the miners said.

"Great. Ye can manage the mine as ye see fit. When I arrive in Florence, I'll have the lawyer at the assayer's office prepare the contract."

Jacob removed the gunbelt from the outlaw as he was coming to. He searched his pockets, found $300, and gave it and the gun rig to the miners as part of their pay. "Gather up their rifles and ammo. You may need to protect the mine. These outlaws won't need any of it where they're going."

"Would ye lend a hand in burying these two thugs?" Rory said, "While the sheriff and I tie this coyote to t' tree for t' night."

Chapter Twelve

NIGHT HAD SETTLED OVER the canyon. They gathered around a crackling fire, the warm glow illuminating their faces. The cabin was well stocked with supplies, and since the earlier meal had been disrupted, they prepared a hearty meal together. The aroma of roasted meat, beans, biscuits, and fresh vegetables mingled with the crisp night air. They mostly sat in silence. The miners discussed their plans for the mine while passing around a bottle of moonshine they found in the cabin, lifting their spirits and fueling their dreams of striking it rich.

Morning came all too soon. "We need tae get a move on; we have much tae do," Rory said. "Ar' ye fellas gonna be all right fir now?" directing his question to the miners.

"No worries, sir. Within' what you made available to us, we can secure the minin' camp and keep it operatin' fir… least a month." Rory shook their hands and then saddled his horse.

The prisoner was cuffed and put on his horse. The posse mounted up. Jacob rode up next to the sheriff. "You spose you can get this one to town and locked up? I'll send Cali along with you. When I was following one of the outlaws to the mine, Apache had crossed his tail and shot him full of arrows."

"Thanks, that'll make it easier with Cali along." The posse split up as Sheriff Payne and Cali traveled northeast along the trail back to town, with the prisoner in tow, while Jacob and Rory headed north through the desert toward the ranch.

Curby and his outlaws rode into Wettin's Four Peaks Ranch. An outlaw led Alisa's horse. With her hands tied, she held onto the saddle horn. When they reached the house an outlaws touched her leg to help her down, she kicked him in the face, causing him to stumble back and fall butt-first onto the ground. He grabbed his nose and cussed something fierce. "Hellacious woman," he yelled out.

"Now, watch your tongue around the woman," Curby said. "We treat her with respect unless the boss says otherwise.

"She busted my nose." Blood was oozing from his nose as he held it, sitting on the ground.

"Be polite and ask first before you touch a lady. Understood? Now, get yourself cleaned up and have Mazewell take a look at it." Giving Alisa a barn sour look, the humiliated hired gun stomped off to find Mazewell.

Mazewell was a ranch hand Wettin had hired. He was good at light work around the ranch yard and buildings, and his skills as a surgeon's nurse and chuck cook in the Confederate Army made him even more helpful.

"Miss Alisa, you had no right to kick him. He was only trying to help," Curby said, looking up at her on the saddle.

"You kidnapped me, tied me up, fed me slop for food, and gave me no privacy. He deserved a kick in the face."

"Fine. Swing your leg around, and I'll help you down." Alisa threw her right leg over the horse while holding the saddle horn. She pulled her boot from the stirrup and dropped to the ground, expecting Curby to catch her. However, as she jumped down, Curby moved aside. She landed on her feet, but the momentum caused her to stumble and fall onto her backside. She yelled in pain and let out a curse in Irish that no one understood. "I'm so sorry, ma'am. Did that hurt? I must have misunderstood. Did you want help down?" Curby couldn't hide the grin on his face.

He reached out his hand to help her off the ground. She pushed it away, pulled up her calico skirt, and with her hands tied, rolled onto her side, then got on one knee and stood. She smiled. "Now, Mister Curby, take me to your leader." Curby followed behind her, shaking his head as she limped toward the ranch house.

Frank Wettin stood at the door to greet them. "Welcome," he said as the two made their way up the steps onto the front porch. "I've been eager to meet you finally, Miss Alisa." Alisa paused in front of him, staring with an expression that could send her Irish hounds running. "Well, okay then, we can get to know each other later. In my house, you are my guest…"

"You mean kidnapped prisoner?" She blurted out.

Wettin was taken aback for a moment. "No… well, yes. Somewhat. You are my prisoner, sure. But you will be treated as a guest while you're in my house. However, I warn you: if you try anything, hurt anyone, or attempt to escape, I will turn you over to my crew— and there are no guarantees about that. Now, I have a room on the second floor ready for you. The window is sealed, and

I have a guard at the front and rear of the house. If you leave the house… again, there are no guarantees. Is that understood?"

Alisa nodded her head. She knew the risks he mentioned. It would be better if she continued to play along, hoping her rescuers would retrieve her soon.

"Oh, good. Here she is. Alisa, this is my housemaid, Agnes. She will show you to your room. She's prepared a bath, laid out a clean dress for you, and has a meal waiting. Curby, take those ropes off her." Curby complied.

Alisa rubbed her wrists where the ropes had chafed her skin. "Sure. I'll be your house guest. I'll eat your food, drink your wine, and stay in your guest room. What you won't get in return is my father giving up his land."

"I have made him more than a fair offer for it. And, as you may know, I get what I want."

"Why do you want the land? You have plenty. Even more than you need for your cattle."

It's not about the cattle, young lady. The day after tomorrow, I'll take you to your father. I told him you were in good condition, so I brought you back here to clean up and look presentable—I wouldn't want your father to think I couldn't care for a lady. When this is finished, you and your family can start fresh somewhere new. Now, if you don't mind. I have work to do." Wettin nodded at his housemaid, and Agnes instructed Alisa to follow.

It was nearly noon, Rory and Jacob rode into the ranch yard with Alisa's riderless horse in tow. They planned to resupply, eat, and rest themselves and the horses before meeting the sheriff and Cali at the turn-off to the Four Peaks Ranch at first light. But mostly to check on Sophia and Henry. After the evening supper, they explained everything that transpired at the outlaw mine camp and their plans for the following day.

Sheriff Payne and Cali arrived late to the rendezvous. "Sorry," Payne said. "I had to get food for the prisoner, hire a guard, and pick up some breakfast and supplies for us."

"It's understood," Rory said. "How well do ye know Wettin's ranch?" he asked Sheriff Payne.

"I've been there a few times with Sheriff Thompson. I never went inside the house, so I only have an understanding of where things are around the ranch."

"Lay it out the best you can," Jacob said.

"The main house is centered in the back between two corrals. Directly behind the house is the garden and tree groves. On the east side, behind the corral, is the carriage house. The bunkhouse and barn are next to the west corral, then the stables are a little further north. Then, a wood fence encircles the property with a gateless entrance at the front."

"How far away do you 'spect the garden and grove of trees are?"

"I'd say, maybe forty feet."

"Is there any cover before you reach the ranch?"

"Yes, there's planted trees all along the property as a snow and windbreak for the winter months."

"Here's the plan," Jacob said. "Since most of the ranch hands and outlaws might be around the bunkhouse and barn, Sheriff, you and Cali cover the area between the bunkhouse and barn. Rory, come with me and cover the carriage house and main house. I'll take Alisa's horse, come in from the garden and tree grove, and enter the rear of the house. Hopefully, any men inside will make their way outside. I will go in and find Alisa. Keep an eye open for me and one on the outlaws. Keep us covered in case we're spotted. Light a shuck when you see us clear the fence and head to our horses. Alisa and I will ride for Pinal and meet you at the sheriff's office. The rest of you ride drag and watch our backs. Any questions?

"They looked at each other. "I think we got it," said Sheriff Payne.

"Alright, let's make our way in. Don't start shooting until you see me heading for the house. If you're spotted, don't return fire until I am in place. We want to keep this as much of a surprise as possible."

The sheriff and Cali split off to the west while Rory and Jacob veered to the east as they approached the ranch. The tree cover was just ten feet from the fence, providing the sheriff and Cali a view of the entrances to both structures and the west corral. Cali focused on the bunkhouse, and Sheriff Payne watched over the barn with a slight view of the back of the house. Rory was in a position to monitor the east corral, the carriage house, and Jacob.

Within moments of reaching their positions, Jacob had crossed the fence into the tree grove. He paused briefly to survey his surroundings. Then, staying low, he quickly approached the house, pressing his back against it near the stairs to the rear door. Rory and Sheriff Payne looked on. All was going as planned. Payne signaled to Cali, and the posse began shooting at the buildings. Rory covered Jacob.

The hired hands were up before sunrise, tending to the horses, and now, they were in the barn for morning chuck. They usually ate before the outlaws, still lying around in the bunkhouse. Startled by gunfire, the outlaws, in their long underwear, jumped from their bunks.

Some put on their boots, but all rushed for their handguns or rifles. When the first one opened the bunkhouse door, wood splintered from Cal's rifle, pushing the outlaws back in.

In the barn, the men quickly stood up from their chuck table, one side knocking over their bench and falling over it. They had left their guns in the bunkhouse for chores and could not fight back.

In the main house, Agnes was about to serve breakfast. Frank and his ranch foreman, Ace Linder, were at the table discussing ranch business. Alisa was about to come down the stairs when the shooting started. She paused. Frank and Ace stood from the table. Agnes had come in from the kitchen. Frank grabbed two rifles and two boxes of ammo from the rifle rack and handed one to Ace. "Keep an eye on her, Agnes," Wettin said, and the two men ran out the front door, crossing over to the nearest water trough along the east corral.

Earlier, while preparing breakfast, Agnes glanced out the window just as a man positioned himself along the side of the house. She was just about to tell Mr. Wettin when she walked into the dining room, and then the rifle fire erupted. She noticed Alisa with a slight smile at the top of the stairs and instantly understood. She placed her food tray on the table and waved at Alisa to come down quickly. She did.

"This way, my dear," Agnes said, leading her to the kitchen's back door. "I'm sorry you had to go through all this. If I hadn't needed this job so badly, I would have left a long time ago. I think someone outside is waiting for you. A handsome young man. Even my tired eyes can see that."

Alisa looked through the door, which was slightly ajar. With his Colt ready, Jacob leaned out to see who had opened the door and saw Alisa peek through. His heart jumped a beat—a feeling he had never experienced before.

"It's Jacob," Alisa said with excitement. He's here. I knew he'd come for me."

"Quickly, go now before we're found out."

"But what about you, Agnes?"

"Don't worry about me, love. I can take care of myself and these bullies. Go now!"

Alisa opened the door and stepped out. Jacob reached up and took her hand. "Stay low and run for the fence and the tree line."

So far, it had been a fortunate rescue. However, by the time the rescue was finished, the outlaws in the bunkhouse had finished getting dressed, and the hands in the barns were nearly done saddling the horses.

Under the bright morning sun, Jacob, Alisa, and Rory kicked up the dust as they charged down the main road toward town. Sheriff Payne and Cali stayed behind to give some distance to the three.

Payne left the barn area and ran over to Cali. "Stay sharp, Cali. Keep the outlaws covered. I'll bring the horses."

Payne rode up with Cali's horse in tow. With a swift motion, Cali swung into the saddle while the horse was still moving, their hoofs pounding before the first outlaw even made it out of the bunkhouse.

Fank Wettin and his foreman never fired a shot. They could only tell that the rifle fire was coming from the west, and they were too far away to help without exposing themselves.

Frank and Ace rushed to the barn as the outlaws exited the bunkhouse. The hired hands were bringing the horses out. "Get after them, whoever they are. Keep at least one alive and bring him back."

"Who do ya 'spose they are?" Ace asked Frank.

"My guess... the McDuncan crew." He stopped and looked at the house, then ran to it. Frank rushed through the front door into the kitchen with Ace behind him.

Agnes wasn't there. He rushed up the stairs as Agnes was coming down. "Is everyone all right? Is anyone hurt?" she asked with sympathy.

"Where is she?" he asked.

"Who? Alisa? I saw her go to her room when the shooting started. I just finished up with your room. I'll go finish breakfast for you two." Wettin pushed her against the wall and rushed up the staircase.

Ace remained at the foot of the stairs. Wettin pounded on the door. Silence. He opened the door and looked inside. Alisa was gone.

Chapter Thirteen

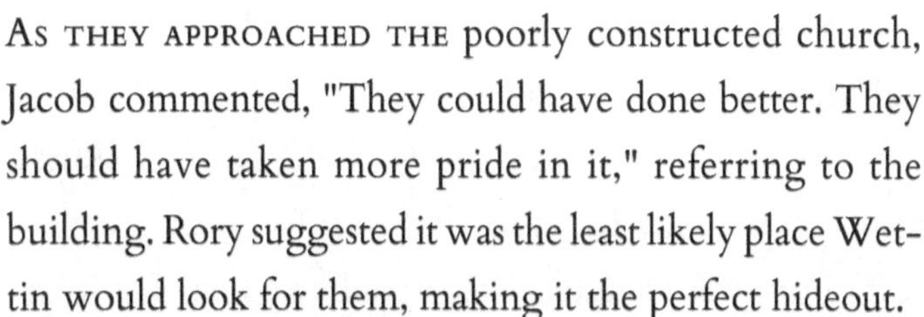

As they approached the poorly constructed church, Jacob commented, "They could have done better. They should have taken more pride in it," referring to the building. Rory suggested it was the least likely place Wettin would look for them, making it the perfect hideout.

"Aye, they were in a right hurry when they were buildin' it, ye know - put it up in a day and a half. It was just more important for them tae get back tae work." Rory remarked, displeased.

Jacob and Alisa stepped off their horses. "I'm leaving you and Rory here. I need to ride back and make sure the sheriff and Cali are all right," Jacob said.

Alisa kissed and hugged him. "Thank you for saving me. That's twice now. And honestly, as exciting as it is, I hope our adventures continue without the threat of danger hangin' over us."

"First off, that's the finest thank you I've ever had, and second, your pa was a true partner in all this. He backed me all the way.

Alisa glanced at her father as he dismounted from his horse. "Oh, he'll get his, too. Now, be careful." She smiled and took her father's arm while Jacob mounted and rode off; Rory and Alisa headed up the steps to the church.

Gunshots echoed in the distance as Jacob approached, he realized he might be riding straight into the midst of the confrontation. He veered off the trail and around a hill, hoping to come up behind the outlaws. He stayed close to the brush as much as he could. He dismounted as he approached the trail, deciding to go on foot the rest of the way. Staying low, he followed alongside the trail until he reached a large, jagged boulder. It offered him a good foothold, allowing him to climb up and look over the surrounding area. Jacob could make out four shooters. They were taking cover within the rocky areas of the hills. He couldn't tell if the sheriff and Cali were kept from reaching their horse to make a run for it, or if the road agents were keeping them from getting to them. The only thing he could do was join the fight.

A bullet ricocheted off the rock, sending pieces of rocky debris into the outlaw's face. It startled and hurt him. "We've got a coyote creeping up on our flank," the man hollered. Just then, another outlaw screamed in pain. Jacob was not taking any chances; he was determined to ensure they would not lose this fight, so he began unloading his weapons at them. It worked. They began to panic as they ran for their horses and mounted up.

"What about Zane?" one of the hired guns asked.

"Nothing we can do unless we all get kilt," another gunman answered.

"He's dead already," the other said. The remaining outlaws kicked their horses into a fast run.

Everything was quiet for a while. Jacob hollered, "Cali, sheriff, it's Jacob. Is anyone hurt?"

"No one is hurt," the sheriff shouted back. "We heard horses. Are the gunmen still around?"

Jacob climbed down and walked along the trail toward his friends. "It's okay, come out. They rode out as fast as when they rode in."

Cali and the sheriff emerged from their hiding place and met Jacob on the open trail. "Gracias, Señor. I'm glad you are here," Cali said as he approached Jacob.

"I'm glad you showed up, too," Sheriff Payne responded. "We had to find some cover fast when they finally caught up. The horses were skittish, an' they cornered us like coyotes huntin' prairie dogs."

"Help me," came a voice somewhere off the trail. The three looked at each other in surprise.

"I thought they all rode out. We must have hit one of them in the shooting."

Jacob signaled, and the men spread out around the area. Having drawn their handguns, they slowly worked around the large rocks.

"Where are you, mister!" Jacob yelled.

He quietly listened, just as he was about to repeat it, a soft voice said, "Help me, please."

Jacob moved to his left, believing the voice came from that direction. He walked about ten feet before spotting legs and boots on the ground sticking out from behind a boulder. "Over here," he hollered. "I've found him." Cali and the sheriff came running.

Jacob slowly moved around the rock, his handgun at the ready. When he peeked around it, he saw the man seated with his back against the rock. He was holding his chest, and his hands and shirt were all bloody.

The wounded outlaw glanced up. "Please, sir, don't shoot me. I'm already kilt… about to get my judgment."

Jacob stepped over him and picked up the pistol on the ground to be cautious. "Mister, I'm sorry you had to go this way."

"I guess we sow what we reap, right?" Looking up, he tried to give Jacob a slight smile but grimaced in pain.

Cali and the sheriff arrived, looking down at the outlaw. "Is he talking?" Sheriff Payne asked.

"Some," Jacob said.

"Mister," the sheriff said. "What's your name? Do you have anyone I can contact for ya?"

"My name? Doesn't matter. I've got no one, no kin. And to beat all heck, the horse I was ridin' wasn't even mine, Nothing worth a plug nickel. I'm heading for Hades, and I reckon... I'll have nothing there, either."

"How about you do one good thing before you go? I'll make sure you get a nice spot up on Boot Hill—put plenty of stones on top so the critters don't get at ya. What ya say?"

The dying outlaw glanced up at the sheriff; his words were getting rough. "What... you need to know?"

"How many hired guns does Wettin have, and what are his plans?"

"Four after I'm gone." The outlaw paused to gather his thoughts. "I overheard him talking in the barn. He said he had business in Tucson and was fixin' to rustle up more gunmen there."

"When's he headed for Tucson?"

The outlaw spoke softly. Sheriff Payne knelt and leaned in to repeat the question. In a whispered tone, the gunman replied, "After he got... McDunkcan's deed."

Payne turned to the hired gun, "How's he getting…" He paused in mid-sentence. The outlaw was dead.

"Cali, can you find the man's horse? The sheriff and I will move him out of the rocks and closer to the trail," Jacob said.

Cali found the horse less than half a mile away, chomping on grass. When he returned, they laid the outlaw belly down over the saddle and tied his hands and feet to keep him secure. The horse was skittish from the smell of blood, but adjusted after a mile on the trail. An hour later, they dismounted in front of the sheriff's office.

"Cali, would you stay here and help the sheriff get him to the coroner's office?" Jacob asked.

"Sî, Señor."

"Thanks. I left Rory and Alisa at the church. I'm gonna ride over and check on them."

"Go ahead," the sheriff said. "Cali and I can handle this." Jacob nodded and turned his horse toward the church.

When Jacob entered the church, all three turned to see who had come in. Alisa jumped up and ran over to him, taking his hand. "Come, I want you to meet the Parson. Reverend Peters, this is my friend Jacob Long.

Reverend Peters is the circuit minister for the local towns and mining camps."

Jacob shook hands with the parson. "Reverend Nolan Peters, it's a pleasure to meet you."

" Please, just Nolan if you'd like."

"Nolan, I didn't realize there were still Circuit Riders. I thought Peters was a German name, but I hear a slight Irish brogue. Weren't all Irish Catholic?"

"Aye, I am some Irish, lad. It's a common name throughout Europe, and tae answer your questions, In Ireland, it's Mac Pheadair, which means Son of Peter. It was changed when my parents came to America, makin' it easier to say and spell. In Northern Ireland, many belong to the Church of Ireland, which is more Protestant. So, with the growth of boom towns from mining, the Church sent out temporary ministers where they could until a permanent church and ministery could be established."

Rory butted in. "Jacob, my boy, we were jus' discussin' with Reverend Peters, here, aboat why we haven't been tae church t' las' few weeks."

Jacob rubbed the back of his neck, feeling uneasy. Deeply religious parents had raised him. Whenever there wasn't a church nearby, his father would hold services at home, which included singing a few songs and reading from the scriptures. He couldn't remember the last time he stepped foot in a church. "Yes," Jacob responded. "I suppose we have been busy. We've been fending off a lot of trouble and worry."

"And that's why ye should be in church," the Parson said, his voice warm and welcoming. "God's Word gives us everythin' we need, so it does. The Bible teaches us we've got many enemies—enemies o' every kind, mind ye. But God is with us in our battles. When we choose faith over fear and worry, we give Him control. If ye let Him, He will guide ye through it all. Remember Psalm 34:4, it says, 'I sought the Lord, and He heard me, and delivered me from all my fears.'"

"I remember my mother reading the Psalms," Jacob said. "I can't recall the scripture about the shadow of death: 'Even though I walk through the valley of the shadow of death, I will fear no evil; for He is with me? I think that's how it goes. "

"No, yer right, that was good, it was. It might seem that when all is lost 'n dark, ye're ridin' beside the shadow o' death, it might. But remember, if we reach out to Him, He's there with us, guidin' us… ridin' alongside us, he is."

Pastor Nolan began to walk away, but stopped and looked over his shoulder slightly. "Ye know, Jacob, the path ye're on today is different from the one ye were on before. God lets ye choose, he does. If ye pick the wrong path, it can take ye so far away... It's a long road home, it is. I just hope ye're not too far down that path."

There was a pause. Jacob was a bit stunned by the pastor's comment. "A *long road home?*" he thought. *How strange it was that two people would use the same line just weeks apart.*

No one knew exactly what to say next. "Well," said the pastor. Lightening the mood. "Now, that wasn't my sermon. That's tomorrow, it is. I expect to see ye all here at eleven sharp, mind you. We'll be havin' a lovely potluck after that."

Jacob let out a long breath after the Parson left. Although his words were hard to hear, Jacob knew he was right. He hadn't been living up to what his parents had taught him. He was grateful they had taught him right from wrong, but he was living life on his own terms. Was it retribution or justice he sought? Deep down, Jacob knew he needed to change. He understood that. Deep down, he knew that if he approached things differently, it might all turn out better for him.

Sheriff LeRoy Payne and Cali sat on the rocking chairs on the boardwalk in front of the sheriff's office. They stood up as Jacob, Alisa, and Rory approached on horseback. Sheriff Payne removed his hat. "Miss Alisa, I'm glad to see you're alright." He put his hat back on his head. Turning his attention to Jacob, "About time."

"I'll have you to know," Jacob said from atop his horse. "It's Saturday, and we've already been to church.

"Well, I'll be." The sheriff slapped his knee. You must have met Reverend Peters. Yes sir. He's a good man of God. Knows his scripture. That's for sure. So, I 'spect I'll be seeing you here for church tomorrow, again?" Sheriff Payne said with a grin and handed Jacob a piece of paper.

Jacob took it. "We've been busy while ya'all been lollygagging," said the sheriff with a playful yet serious look. So, what's this?" He took a moment to look at it. "A wanted poster?"

"The fella we brought in is Jebidiah Boone. He has a $500 bounty on his head for armed robbery and for puttin' a bullet in a bank clerk out in Kansas Territory. Since you took him down, the reward is yours. I will arrange for the bank to draw the funds, and they will notify Kansas for reimbursement."

"No, can't do that," Jacob said. "You an' Cali had as much to do with keepin' them road agents off our backs, so we'll split it three ways."

Cali, all smiles, vigorously shook Jacob's hand. *"Gracias, mucho gracias, señior."*

Thanks, Jacob. Sheriff Payne added, shaking Jacob's hand. "Justice may be slow in these parts, but it sure comes with a price."

Chapter Fourteen

Frank Wettin sat behind his desk, looking out his office window and slowly rocking in his chair. His elbow rested on the armrest, and his chin was supported by his forefinger and thumb, deep in thought.

Just when he thought the end of his scheme was in sight, the ground seemed set to crumble beneath his boots. He leaned back in his creaky chair releasing a weary sigh that hung heavy in the air. He had lost track. It had been seven or eight years since he crossed the threshold of thirty, yet now he felt like a man well into his twilight years, burdened by the weight of too many years running from the law. "What have I done wrong?" he said aloud, turning his chair to gaze at a painting on the wall; the city of New York. At that moment, the city's busy streets and endless possibilities felt like a distant memory, as if they belonged to another lifetime.

Left to live as a street orphan, his father, an excessive drinker, was stabbed to death in a saloon brawl when he was ten. He and his mother worked various jobs to make ends meet, but it wasn't enough. When he turned twelve, he and his mother were forced out of their squalid apartment for a higher-paying tenant. This area in New York was known as Five Points, which would later become Chinatown. Located on Manhattan's Lower East Side, it was a dangerous slum for poor immigrants, consisting of rundown wooden and brick shacks, buildings, businesses, and warehouses. Groves of English, German, Welsh, Scots, and Irish refugees began flooding in by the 1840s. Saloons, gambling houses, opium dens, and brothels were numerous, a breeding ground for criminal activity and gangs.

The young man and his mother stood resolutely in the warm afternoon light near the front of the deteriorating tenement building. At 27, her face bore the marks of a hard-earned life. "You're a man now, son," she said, her voice trembling, mixed with regret and sorrow. She pressed three crumpled dollars into his palm, each wrinkled bill a testament to their shared struggles. Their history was apparent in that small gesture, a reminder of the taxing battles fought in the slums of poverty. She knelt to tighten the cord that held her suitcase closed. She brushed his hair and winked at him. Trying to reassure him. A tear rolled down his cheek as she blended into the bustling crowd on the streets. He stood in front of the tenement building, feeling an overwhelming sense of loss and loneliness. His only possessions were a few worn clothes bundled in an old towel with frayed edges.

For two weeks, he was careful with his few dollars, resorting to begging on the streets and sleeping in alleys. Living in this corrupt world called Five Points, where five streets converged, he learned to stash his bills in his sock and keep only a few coins in his pocket. It wouldn't be long before older street Arabs robbed him, a term used for street orphans who constantly roamed the streets, avoiding capture and sent west on the orphan train.

The young man was determined to find work, so he approached a merchant one day to inquire about available job opportunities. However, the merchant shooed him away. As he headed for the door, he considered taking a piece of fruit from a nearby basket but ultimately decided against it and walked out. Unbeknownst to him, a customer was watching. Sitting on the curb of the dusty dirt road, he rested his head on his knees. Behind him, a man stood. "So, tell me, young master, why didn't you steal the orange from the basket? The merchant wasn't even in the room."

He looked up at the man. "Because I want to pay for it on my own. If I steal, it'll become too easy to keep doing it, and I'll never amount to anything. My mother would always tell me that."

"You have a strong spirit, principles, and determination to succeed, A true American, laddie. Unlike those not born here an' only live for the moment, I do say."

"Aw, I ain't quite sure what all that gobbledygook means," he said, scratching his head. "Thank ye kindly, sir... Is there anythin' I can do for ya, sir?"

"Yes, since you speak honestly, and I presume you wouldn't steal from me since you didn't steal that orange, correct?"

"I would not, sir."

"What's your name, lad?"

"Gunther, sir."

"Good German name, Gunther. Your parents are German?"

"My father was, sir. He's dead."

"And your mother?"

"They never told me what country she came from. Irish, I think. She left me. I don't know where she is."

"Well, that's just too bad. But maybe it's good for me. Do me a favor, kid. Here's a quarter. Be a good *nipper*, run down the block, and get me a newspaper.

Bring it to that saloon over there on the corner called the Bank Exchange. Tell them it's for William," he pointed. "They'll know. Now hurry."

Gunther stood and took the coin. "Yes, sir, right away." Then he headed for the next block. A few minutes later, he walked through the door of the saloon. He walked up to the nearest man leaning against the bar. "Mister, I've got the paper Mr. William's asked me to get for him.

The man momentarily looked down at Gunther. "He did, did he?" The kid nodded his head. "Alright, he's in the back room," pointing to a door in the back. "By the way, kid, that's William Poole. He owns this joint and leader of the Bowery Boys, so don't sass him. He'll box your ears. Got it?"

"Mr. Poole, it is. Yes, sir. I got it." Gunther opened the door to the back room and called for Mr. Poole.

"Who is it?"

"It's Gunther, Mr. Poole. I have yer paper, sir."

"Great, bring it back here." William Poole was seated at a round table with two other gentlemen. "Boys, I'd like you to meet Gunther." The two men just looked at him.

Gunther handed him the paper, then dug into his pocket. "And yer change, sir," he added, holding out his hand.

"Na, you keep it. You earned it. You were honest and didn't run off with my quarter." Gunther put it back in his pocket. "How would you like to make more than the few cents in your pocket, Gunther?"

"I would sir, yes."

"I need someone I can trust to run errands and keep an eye on things around the Five Points."

From then on, he started running errands, making deliveries, and acting as a spy for the Bowery Boys. Later, William provided Gunther with a shoe-shining kit and a stool. His job involved infiltrating areas controlled by rival gangs, shining their shoes, and listening to conversations.

As a shoeshine boy, he appeared inconsequential to the arrogant men around him, allowing them to speak freely while he polished their shoes and boots. The best part was that William paid him for any valuable information he gathered, and he was allowed to keep his earnings and tips. Gunther was given a small room above the saloon, and as his wealth grew, he deposited his income into a bank outside the slum area of Five Points.

In 1855, when Gunther was fourteen, William Poole was gunned down by a rival political member. He was only 34. The Bank Exchange Saloon was closed down. Poole's wife allowed Gunther to continue living above the saloon for a fraction of what rent would cost elsewhere until she decided what she wanted to do with the saloon.

Gunther continued with Poole's Bowery Boys until they disbanded around 1865. Some left the area without a strong leader, while more hardened criminals joined other gangs.

Months later, Gunther was recruited into the Whyos gang. Their method was to recruit young men under the guise of joining a family, and Gunther was one of them. By the time he turned 25, he was managing the protection service that the family provided to vendors and shops. If shops failed to pay their monthly premium, either their shop, cart, or booth would receive a visit, resulting in theft and destruction that would be blamed on local thieves or rival gangs. This made their protection policy seem credible. His salary was based on a percentage of the earnings. His ethical values shifted as he accumulated a small fortune.

One day, he made a life-changing mistake: he agreed to help rob a bank in New York City's financial district. Convinced by other gang members that it would be an easy in-and-out job, the organizers believed their source was trustworthy. They were, however, set up.

The rise of organized crime had become so rampant that law enforcement agencies started to become strategic in their methods of putting a stop to the gangs. The gang's reliable source informed the police about the time and location of the bank robbery. Just as the thieves thought they had secured their loot; police sirens pierced the air. When the police arrived at the front of the building, the gang members inside panicked and began firing from within the bank. Amid the chaos, Gunther ducked into a back room with a portion of the loot he was to carry, all tied up within a white cloth bank bag.

The room he was in served as a break room for employees and also functioned as the back entrance to the bank. Gunther noticed a leather satchel on the floor under a bench. He took it and dumped the cash from the bank bag into it. At the rear of the room was a metal door. Pulling back the bolt lock he opened it carefully, peeking outside, but saw no one there. Exiting the building, he headed around the back. Just as he was about to round the corner, someone shouted, "Stop! Police!" Gunther turned, still in panic mode, and not thinking, instinctively fired his weapon. It felt like slow motion as he saw a young policeman grab his chest, drop his gun, and fall to his knees before lying face down on the ground. Gunther stood in silence and shock tuning out all the gunfire and chaos surrounding him. When his senses returned—he turned and ran.

The finality felt like a distant memory of a forgotten dream. Hours later, he sat on the edge of his bed in the dim light of his room. A weight of unease settled over him. He couldn't shake thoughts of impending betrayal. In seeking self-preservation, he knew it was only a matter of time before one of the gang members would betray him, possibly even naming him the ringleader to save their skins. As he lay down, he put his hands behind his head; he needed to think. He could turn himself in, but he would only end up convicted and hanged. He concluded he had to leave New York.

Throughout the long night, Gunther packed his few belongings and devised his plan. The following day, just before dawn, when the streets were mostly empty, he carefully left the Five Points district. His first stop was the livery stables, where he bought a horse, tack, and gear. In the horse stall, he packed his belongings into the pommel saddle bags. He stashed his stolen money in the leather cantle saddle bag, tucked his handgun into his waistband, and buttoned his jacket. Slinging the leather saddlebag he purchased over his shoulder; he left the stall to find the owner.

After arranging with the livery owner to hold his horse, he walked to the mercantile on the next block. Purchasing a revolver and holster rig, he added a repeating rifle, ammunition, a saddle scabbard for the rifle, camping, sleeping, cooking gear, and other supplies for his journey; he informed the store clerk that he would be back later to retrieve them. He had one final bit of business to attend to: closing his bank account. The fact that he had kept the account a secret all these years meant no one would be looking for him there. He thanked the banker, put the cash into his saddlebag, and exited the bank.

Over the years, he drifted westward through every dusty two-bit cow town and mining camp, refining his skills as a thief, cunning conman, liar, and cheat. By the time he reached the sunbaked landscapes of Arizona, he was a trail-hardened outlaw. Everything had changed. He was a different man now—he was Frank Wettin.

Chapter Fifteen

THE BOTTOMER'S SALOON WAS alive with the raucous sounds of a boom town echoing through the rustic wooden beams. It was near evening, and the lanterns flickered their dim light against the walls. Boots clacked on the weathered floorboards, mingling with the low murmur of hushed conversations and the occasional burst of laughter from miners spending their hard earnings. The melodic fingering of a Spanish guitar resonated from the corner, accompanied by the rhythmic clinking of whiskey glasses and the faint shuffling of cards dealt at the nearby tables. At the back of the saloon, a group of ranchers, their faces weathered by the sun, gathered around a large oval table. Their voices rose and fell as they debated cattle prices, recent horse trades, and concerns over Frank Wettin. Amidst it all, the bartender shouted orders while the swinging batwing doors creaked as patrons entered and exited, adding to the saloon's lively discord.

Two men entered and paused, scanning the room. "Over here," hollered one of the ranchers, waving his arm above the noise of the busy saloon.

Jacob and Rory walked over to the table. Five ranchers sat around holding whisky and beer glasses, and a few puffed on cigars. "Why, aren't we a sorry bunch of canny-lookin' cowboys th't I've ever seen?" Rory said to the bunch.

"Who are you buttering up to, ya old Irish coot? Are ya's runnn' for county office or something?" One of the ranchers blurted back with a grin on his face.

"Na, tryin' to make up for the cattle that turned their backs on ye las' time ye was at the ranch." Rory blurted back.

"Why'd they do that?" another rancher asked.

"They said they was in the mood for intellect, not nonsense!" The men chuckled around the table. The good-natured ribbing lightened the mood.

Rory pulled out the chair and sat down. Jacob did the same. "Glad ye all made it," Rory said. "Ah, this fella here is Jacob Long. He's a great pal and has been a huge help in sorting things out with Wettin." The ranchers nodded their greetings. "Sure, as ye all know, that scoundrel Wettin took me daughter, tryin' to force me hand to sign over the deed tae me ranch. "We tracked her down to Wettin's place, and by force, we took her back yesterday; thank the heavens above. She's doin' all right!" The ranchers let out a breath of relief.

"What are we goin' to do about it?" a rancher asked. "Wettin's harassin' Tom and Clancy for the deeds to their place, and the other three of us are fearin' he may do the same."

Tom cleared his throat, his voice steady but tinged with concern. "Clancy and I are just simple ranchers—ain't but our families tending to the land. We don't have the means to hire hands or gunmen to watch our backs. Just last week, the low-down skunks drove Baker off his land, givin' 'em a pittance for it; we're struggling to hold our ground."

"We understand that, Jacob said. "We've been told that Frank Wettin left today for Florence and Tucson. He plans to file his deeds and register a bogus mining claim on Rory's land. However, he secured a letter from the Silver King Mine, permitting him to mine in the Pioneer Mining District. After the meeting, we're fixin' to ride out in the morning for Tucson, contact the assayer's office lawyer, and inform the marshal of his activity."

"Ah, sure, let's hope we can stop him once and for all," Rory said. "Sheriff Payne has penned a letter detailing his involvement and kidnappin' and askin' the marshal's office fer a warrant tae have him arrested. It's high time we end this if'n ye ask me."

"From what we know, he's down to just four hired guns," Jacob added, "and I reckon a couple of 'em will stick by him to keep him safe. My hunch is you won't have too much trouble while he's away. But let me tell ya, don't go thinkin' you can let your guard down just yet,"

The ranchers engaged in small talk, but there wasn't much else to say. As much as they wanted to complain about it, they held back their tongues.

Just before dawn, three men departed from the Four Peaks Ranch. Their horses were given their heads, eager to be on the trail. Sensing the anticipation of adventure, they eagerly tossed their manes and shifted their weight. The Arizona morning was cool and invigorating. A gentle breeze infused the fresh scent of damp foliage, a lingering fragrance left by the light rain that had fallen overnight.

The surroundings became more vibrant as the sun rose, casting a warm golden glow across the landscape. The once-muted colors burst into rich greens as the moisture revitalized the flora. Dotted along the trail, the striking Palo Verde trees, with their distinctive blue-green bark, stood out vividly against the backdrop of the sandy terrain. Surrounding them were Desert Willow trees, their slender branches adorned with delicate, willow-like leaves, swaying gently in the breeze, while the Ocotillo plants were beginning to showcase their striking red tubular flowers, a promise of the blooming season ahead.

In the distance, proud and steadfast, the majestic Saguaro Cacti rose against the sapphire sky, their many uniquely shaped arms creating a breathtakingly picturesque scene. Each cactus stood as a testament to the resilience of life in this arid landscape, offering a stunning contrast to the vibrant colors of the morning.

"We're making good time, men," said Frank Wettin, the owner of the Four Peaks Ranch. "At this pace, we'll make Florence by noon. We'll grab a quick bite at the café, then I have some business. Duke, I need you to rustle up at least four hired guns. Offer 'em the cash advance with the balance after the job, but make sure they they have the grit to see this through, then report back to me. I'll need them at the livery and ready to ride at first light tomorrow. Reed, you stick with me."

"Yes, sir," Reed replied.

An hour before noon, the three rode up to the hitching rail outside the local café in Florence. They dismounted and secured the reins around the wooden rails. Stepping onto the boardwalk, Frank paused to look around before entering the cafe. The café was spacious enough to accommodate the many miners and business travelers, with numerous stagecoach companies arriving daily.

It was sunup when Duke and the four hired guns rode up to the livery. "We're saddled and ready to ride, boss," he said as he dismounted."

"Alright then. Swing by the mercantile and gather what supplies you require. Put it on my tab; I'll settle with the clerk before I ride to Tucson. I have a meeting with a business associate today. Feel free to grab some breakfast, but I'd like to see you on the trail within the hour."

"Yes, sir, boss."

"And Duke, you know the description of the rascals we're huntin'. Keep a sharp eye peeled. If you lay eyes on 'em, don't hesitate to handle it."

"Understood, boss."

The dusty light flickered over the room, casting shadows that danced like old ghosts. "I reckon it's a rough world out there," Nash Pickett said, the man financing Frank Wettin's take over of the ranches and mining operations.

"Rough indeed," Frank replied, swirling the whiskey in his glass as the two men sat at the bar table. "But it's also ripe for the picking. You see, these ranchers out here think they're in control of the land. But what they don't know is that a little pressure can turn the tide in our favor."

Nash leaned in; his voice low. "What's the plan then? We can't just muscle them off. These folks are stubborn and have neighbors who might not take kindly to our tactics."

Frank smirked. "Stubborn? No, they haven't been, except for one. Rory McDuncan. He and his associate Jacob Long have been a thorn in my side. However, I don't think we have too much to worry about. I have four men ridin' hard. Their task is to remove the thorns.

And, for those who are stubborn, we get creative. We'll start with the water by damming it off with explosives up in the mountain pass. Plant some rumors of a drought and the creek drying up. Once they're rattled, we swoop in with offers for their land—the kind they can't refuse. They'll see it as a chance for quick cash."

"But what if they don't bite?" Nash asked, a hint of doubt creeping into his tone.

Frank waved dismissively. "If they don't bite, we'll apply more pressure and a few well-placed threats. Maybe a barn burns down—It's just enough to convince them that it's unsafe to remain there. And if that doesn't work, well, there are options for the more unsavory type of business, if you catch my meaning."

Nash paused, considering Frank's words. "You mean—"

"I mean, sometimes you've got to take extreme measures," Frank interrupted, his eyes narrowing. "This isn't a game for the faint-hearted. You do what's necessary to get what you want."

Nash rubbed his chin, weighing the moral implications. "And if it comes back on us? These ranchers could rally, especially if we push too hard."

Frank leaned back, a confident smile creeping across his face. "Let them rally. They tried before with no results. With their land and mining profits in our pockets, we can afford to hire more guns. Besides, law enforcement is stretched thin with the marshal busy with all the mining issues, Apaches, and stagecoach robberies. We'll make our move while the iron's hot."

"Alright," Nash finally said, nodding slowly. "If we're going to do this, we must be smart about it. Silence is key. No loose tongues. And we watch our backs—we don't want any rancher or wannabe hero coming after us when the dust settles."

"That's why I'm heading for Tucson when I'm finished here. Get the deeds and mine registered. It'll be a start for our new empire." Frank raised his glass in a toast. "To opportunity, Nash. Let's make sure we capitalize on it before anyone knows what hit them."

Nash clinked his glass against Frank's, echoing ominously in the saloon like a warning bell. The shadows deepened around them as they plotted, the weight of their intentions hanging in the air like storm clouds ready to burst.

Chapter Sixteen

RORY AND JACOB SADDLED up and hit the trail at sunrise. Meanwhile, Henry, Cali, Alisa, and Sophia stayed behind at the ranch, taking turns at the night watch for three or four days. Henry and Cali had moved the cattle to a new grazing area with enough water to satisfy them for a week or more.

Rory pulled out his pocket watch, a family heirloom from his father. He kept it on a gold chain with a hematite pendant in his waistcoat pocket. He opened it. "We've been on the trail for four hours. If we keep this steady pace, we should be in Florence in two and a half hours."

Jacob reined his horse to a sudden stop and stared east. Rory turned his horse around and rode up beside him. "What's the trouble, lad?"

"Do my eyes deceive me, or do I actually see a couple of camels there in the distance," pointing to the side of a distant hill.

Rory put his hands over his eyes to shade them from the sun. "Aye, ye sure do, lad. There's still a wee few of them about. Not that ye see them too often, mind ye. Mostly down in the lower flats near the springs, where there's plenty o' water and lush vegetation."

"What in tarnation are camels doing in Arizona?" giving Rory a dumbfounded look.

"Well, me lad, that's a bonnie tale. When they built the smelter down in Florence, there was a bloke they called Hi Jolly, and he brought in twenty camels he'd bought from the mines in Nevada, ya see."

"What were they used for?"

"I'm not quite sure, to be honest. I think at one point, t' military used 'em as pack animals in the deserts, stretchin' all the way from Texas to California. Aye, but that didn't last long. They ended up sellin' every last one of 'em, scatterin' 'em all over t' territory. I reckon that's how he came by 'em. Brought 'em here to haul silver to the smelter in Florence, but that didn't pan out either. The rocks and stones on the trails were hard on their wee feet. They tried various things to make it work, but everythin' they attempted just fell flat. So lad, they just set 'em free.

And well, there they are," he said, gesturin' off toward the desert.

"And that's how facts become tall tales and legends," Jacob said as he spurred his horse on. Rory turned and followed.

It was no more than an hour later when Jacob reined his horse in again. "Rory, I'm a bit uneasy seeing the dust cloud ahead of us."

"Aye, it could be a right few things, ye know? Might be an ore wagon train comin' back from the smelter in Florence. If it's pulled by eighteen oxen, there'd be plenty of dust flyin' about, I tell ye. Or could be that McDonald Stage Coach Line, runnin' thrice a week between Florence, Pinal, and Silver King. They've got six fine horses that usually make good time, so ye can be sure that'd be kickin' up a fair bit of dust as well!"

"Okay. But…. what about the dust to the east?" He reached around and pulled the looking glass from his saddle bag which Rory had lent him. He studied it for a moment. "Apahces! Comin' right at us!"

"We best kick spur lad and make a run for it!"

A mile down the dirt road, Duke and his hired guns watched the same dust cloud rising in the east, suspecting it was an Apache raiding party. Their best option was to try to outrun them, so they spurred their steeds into a quick run.

As each group ran for it, the dust they spotted ahead on the dirt road and to the east was thickening and getting closer.

Within minutes, the speeding riders noticed one another. Jacob was the first to recognize the front rider, one of Wettin's hired guns. His mixed Cherokee blood stood out from the rest. This gunman, along with his timid riding partner, had previously claimed to be surveying the McDuncan ranch when he and Alisa encountered them in the hills.

They pulled on the reins and stopped. Duke and his riders slowed and came to a halt within twenty feet. "Boys, those are the snakes we're after. Let's get 'em!" The gunmen pulled their pistols, but Jacob and Rory were ready. They turned their horses. They knew their best hope was to get close to the Indians on their trail.

Rory and Jacob veered off the road and headed east into the desert. The immediate challenge was to avoid the cacti and prickly brush while traveling at high speed. They had a simple plan, or so they believed. "When we see the Apache turn south, we'll find cover in the hills!" Jacob yelled out.

The hostiles were spotted on the horizon just moments after their last discussion. They turned south and headed toward a rugged gully where a meandering creek flowed lazily. The uneven ravine offered numerous nooks and crannies perfect for concealment and deepened as they made their way in. As they became more familiar with their location, they decided to venture further in toward the end of the gully, where the landscape opened up into a sprawling valley. When they reached the opening, Jacob pulled his rifle from the saddle scabbard and dismounted. "Rory, take the horses further into the rocks. I'll hold them off."

Crouched low, Rory worked his way through the rocky terrain, hobbled the horses, and carefully returned to Jacob. They spotted the hired guns entering the mouth of the ravine. Midway through their descent, the sharp crack of gunfire rang out, echoing off the canyon walls. One of the outlaws struck in the leg let out a pained cry as he lost his balance. His horse bucked nervously beneath him. With a grimace, he dismounted and limped toward a massive boulder that loomed nearby, using it for cover. The others followed. The last gunman to dismount, undeterred, took aim and fired a volley of rounds from his pistol, returning fire to fend off their attackers from the shadows of the canyon.

After nearly ten minutes of sporadic gunfire, Rory pointed, "There, see 'em, on the ridge."

"I do, but they don't see us. And look, they're working their way along the creek bottom." Just then, arrows started flying from the ridge of the deep gully.

"Aye, it's high time we lit a shuck lad, an' fast," Rory said, his accent rolling over the words.

Amid the chaos of the Indian assault, the hired gunmen were shooting and moving about, deflecting arrows; they lost track of the two men they were pursuing. Their gunfire echoed against the rugged canyon walls. Seizing the moment, Rory and Jacob dashed toward their waiting horses, a pair of powerful steeds with coats glistening under the warm afternoon sun. As they quickly mounted, the horses whinnied and stomped, sensing the adrenaline in the air. With a fierce kick to their flanks, they sprang from their concealment at a run, hooves driving through the creek, splashing and kicking up sand in their wake.

Their plan had worked. Drawing the outlaws into the ravine and blocking the exit with gunfire bought time for the Apache to make their attack from the rear, allowing Jacob and Rory the opportunity to slip away from the clutches of both the Apache and the relentless outlaws. It was a tale of narrow escapes and audacious bravery they would recount in years to come, a story they would share in the future with little need for embellishment.

Three hours later, they arrived in Florence and made their way to one of the two livery stables on the edge of town. Despite being a relatively new town, Florence appeared much older due to eight years of dust, weathering, and hastily constructed buildings. Established in 1866 as an agricultural community by Civil War veteran Levi Ruggles, Florence quickly became the main crossroads for all routes leading to the silver mines in this area of Arizona. Soon, the railroad would also arrive in this region.

"I'll take care of the horses and gear, Rory. If you want to find the town sheriff and see if the Territorial Marshal is around, I'll meet you there as soon as I finish." Rory dismounted and made his way up Main Street while Jacob took the reins and led the horses into the livery.

The livery owner exited his office as Jacob, towing the horses, walked in. "Howdy, mister. What can I do fer ya today?"

"Just need to board the horses for the day. We had some injun and outlaw trouble on the way and worked the horses pretty good. I'd be obliged if you'd take good care of them for me."

"Like my own," the livery owner said. He took the reins from Jacob. "I'm Elmer. Go on, now, take care of business. I'll tend to the horses and gear. They're safe here."

Jacob headed for the livery barn entrance but then stopped and turned back. "Elmer," he said. Elmer peeked his head from a stall. "I was looking for a rancher from the Superstition area named Frank Wettin. Have you seen or heard of him? He should have been in town for a few days."

"Ya, I've heard of him and seen him too… he a friend of yours?"

"No, I wouldn't say that. Not one bit."

"Good. He's a mean cuss. Belly-aching about every little thing and not a lick of decency."

"Is he still around?"

"No, stabled his horse here, though—too much trouble. Next time, I'll tell him to go across the way to Billy's place." He mumbled something about some bad dealings under his breath and about heading to Tucson, the capital building, yesterday.

"Thank you kindly, Elmer," Jacob said, touching his finger to his hat. Elmer ducked back into the stall to finish his work.

When Jacob arrived at the sheriff's office, Rory sat in a chair by the desk. "Here he is," Rory said. "Sheriff, this here is Jacob Long. Jacob, this is Sheriff Rhett Buford."

"Pleased to meet you, sheriff," Jacob said, the sheriff stood to shake his hand.

"I hear you've been a bit of help for Rory here?" the sheriff replied.

Glancing at Rory, "Well, as much as I can be, I guess."

"I was just tellin' Rory that the Territorial Marshal's due into town the day after tomorrow. He's currently held up in Tucson but aims to swing by Pinal and check on the mines as well. Might take him four, maybe five days, dependin' on any ruckus that comes up along the way."

"Has Rory filled you in, Sheriff?"

"He has, and I'm sorry for your troubles."

"Elmer at the Florence Livery said Frank Wettin was in town and left yesterday," Jacob said.

"That coyote slipped away again," Rory said, slapping his hand on his knee.

"Elmer thinks he's headed for the Capitol building in Tucson," Jacob said.

"If'n you'd like, I could wire over a message for the sheriff's office and the capital in Tucson. Let 'em know the interim sheriff of Pinal is requesting a warrant on Frank Wettin for kidnapping, extortion, and falsifying deeds and mining claims. That outta cause him a belly-ache. Are ya trailing him?" Sheriff Buford drawled, tipping his hat back as he leaned against the weathered wall of his office.

"We are," Jacob said.

"But first, our horses need a wee res', an' we need to take a breather, in deed?" Rory said in a tired voice, wiping a bead of sweat from his brow. "We're plumb wore oot ridin' hell-bent from Wettin's hired gunmen an' Apache renegades. We'll get some rooms, an' grub. Then head oot at first light."

The midday sun beat down mercilessly on the dusty town of Florence. They stepped out of the office, the sheriff behind them leaning against the open door. Little clouds of dirt swirled by. Sheriff Rhett nodded, the lines on his weathered face deepening as he considered Rory's words. "Good luck to you then," he said, adjusting his wide-brimmed hat to shield his eyes from the glare. "I'll be sure to inform the sheriff of your arrival. He should be expectin' you. Make it a point to see him first thing in the mornin'. He's got a way of knowing how to make sense of this mess."

Rory shook the sheriff's hand, and Jacob tipped his hat, his gaze sharp as he surveyed the town square. The sound of boots echoed on wooden boardwalk planks, the distant murmur of townsfolk, and the creaky sway of saloon doors filled the air. "I hope it all works out, and again, I'm mighty sorry for your troubles."

Rory and Jacob stepped off the boardwalk and mounted their horses while the sheriff headed for the telegraph office. The tense atmosphere of the town felt thick, like the weight of an approaching storm. Both men knew that the battles they faced were far from over. Jacob lowered his hat to shield his eyes from the sun's glare and adjusted his revolver slightly on his hip as they turned their mounts toward the livery. They needed a plan, but first, they needed rest.

Chapter Seventeen

THE SUN HUNG LOW over the dusty streets of the small Arizona town, casting long shadows as three riders trotted in from the south. Duke, a lean, ruthless mix-breed. His beaded leather tassels adorned his clothing and moccasins, a gunman with a sharp gaze and a Colt revolver slung low on his hip, led the way. His two new companions, Cal and Mose, flanked him—Cal with a scruffy beard and worn duster, Mose broad-shouldered and silent, cradling a Winchester rifle. Their tired horses kicked up dry earth as they slowed near the saloon, eyes scanning the ramshackle buildings for their targets. Duke was furious. Of the four newly hired guns, only he and two others remained. They had been tricked into an ambush with the Apaches; he vowed to take revenge.

"Keep sharp, boys," Duke muttered, spitting tobacco into the dirt. "Rory's no greenhorn, and Long's got a nose for trouble. They fooled us once. It won't happen again."

They secured their weary horses to the worn post railing, its surface rough and splintered from years in the Arizona sun. As they stepped onto the boardwalk, they surveyed the dusty street and the old wooden buildings that flanked it, their sun-bleached paint peeling in the heat. They were exhausted from their fight and ride back, but more than anything, a parched feeling tugged at their throats; this desperation drove them toward the saloon's open door, where the enticing smell and sounds promised strong drinks.

After enjoying a fine breakfast of steaks, potatoes, and eggs, washed down with steaming hot coffee, Jacob and Rory stepped out onto the boardwalk from the café. "Ah've got to head o'er to the Federal Land Management office. See if Wettin filed a claim, Rory said. "I'll meet ye at the mercantile. Be sure to grab the supplies we need, and put them on my account, will ye lad?"

The three hired guns lingered in the dim light of the saloon, cradling their drinks as the smoky air swirled around them. Through the night, they dozed fitfully between sips of fiery whiskey, the clinking of glasses, and the scraping of chairs on the worn wooden floor. When they finally staggered out into the crisp morning air, their spirits were lifted, emboldened by the burn of the liquor coursing through their veins; they felt a bit more daring and fuller of promise. "Okay, boys. Time to get even. Keep a sharp eye." They fanned out, boots drumming against the planked boardwalk. It didn't take long to spot their targets—Rory, tough and sun-browned, sat in a rocker outside the mercantile store while Jacob added supplies to their saddle packs.

Duke tipped his hat low, signaling them with a flick of his fingers. "Cal, take the alley. Mose, up on the roof. We'll force the move and pen 'em in by the livery."

Cal grinned, slipping into the narrow gap between buildings, while Mose hauled himself up a rickety ladder to the mercantile store's roof, rifle in tow. Duke sauntered down the street, hands loose at his sides, watching Rory and Jacob from the corner of his eye. The ambush was set.

It started with a shout. Rory's head snapped up as Cal stepped from the alley, pistol drawn. "This is for ambushing us with the Apache, you sorry bast..."

Jacob interrupted as his gun burst from his holster and fired off three rounds toward the voice. Cal quickly ducked back into the alley.

As the shots cracked through the air. Duke ducked behind a water trough across the street from the Livery stable. Rory and Jacob ran for better cover and away from their horses. The Livery next door offered cover. Rory rolled behind a barrel while Jacob traded lead with Cal, bullets splintering wood and pinging off metal.

Mose, perched above, fired a round from his rifle that grazed Jacob's arm. Jacob ducked into the livery, pressing his back against the wall to inspect the injury. His sleeve was torn where the bullet had grazed him. Quickly, he pulled out his bandana and tied it around the wound.

The sheriff rushed out of the telegraph office. Grabbing the telegraph clerk's 12-gauge shotgun, he burst from the office and ran along the boardwalk towards the sound of gunfire. The early morning risers were up and standing on the boardwalk when the shooting began. Sheriff Rhett waved at them to get inside as he passed them by. He stopped and leaned behind a wide post holding up the roof that covered the boardwalk. From his position, he could see Rory and Jacob by the livery and Duke behind the water trough on his side of the street. He was about to step out from behind the post to take a shot at Duke when the sound of a rifle barked just above him. He watched Jacob grab his arm, ducking into the Livery.

Sheriff Rhett looked up, realizing a shooter was on the roof above him. Duke hadn't seen him. He was busy taking shots at the livery and the barrel Rory was behind. Taking a risk, he carefully moved out into the street, his shotgun raised and ready. It didn't take a moment for Mose to stand up to take a shot at Rory, and as he did, the shotgun let out an explosion from both barrels. The spray of pellets tore into the roof railing and Mose. He dropped his rifle as he slowly leaned forward, falling to the roof cover of the boardwalk face down, knocking dirt and dust off the roof, his lifeless arm dangling over its edge.

Duke quickly turned his gun toward the shotgun blast and fired two quick rounds at Sheriff Rhett, who was still standing in the street. He laughed as he shouted, "Should've stayed outta this, lawman; now you've got a bellyache for breakfast!"

With his left hand, Sheriff Rhet held his side. Pulling his six-shooter, he yelled, "I've buried worse men than you, you mangy cur!" The sheriff advanced, trading fire with Duke, but another slug caught him in the shoulder. Rhett staggered; his handgun fell to the dirt. He worked his way into the alley of the mercantile and slumped against the side of a wagon waiting to be loaded, clutching the wound, he called out. "Sorry, men…I'm hit hard," he rasped, "out of the fight."

The battle spilled toward the livery and livestock yard. Firing at the outlaws, Jacob gave cover for Rory to move into the livery. They retreated out the back of the livery as the gunmen pressed them. Working around the fences that held a herd of cattle to be driven to Tucson and the silver mines south near Bisbee. They kept low.

Duke and Cal followed them into the livery and leaned against the side walls of the rear barn doors, peeking out to see if they could locate the two they hunted. "You take the right. Work your way around, and we'll flank them on both sides," Duke said as he used his gun to point to the right. "I'll cover you, then I'll head out."

Duke waited while Cal reached the corral fencing. No shots had been fired, so Duke ran to the left, staying low. He worked his way along the white picket fence, peeking over the top and firing a round or two, trying to provoke return fire from his rivals. Cal followed suit. Jacob and Rory were pinned behind the corral fencing as the gunmen closed in. Bullets chewed the wood around them as each other's return fire grew sporadic.

Knowing the two outlaws would need to stand to shoot over the bawling cattle, he stood up and waited. When Duke peeked over, Jacob was ready. He fired two rounds, hitting the wood in front of Duke's face and splattering him with shards of fencing. He yelled in pain as he ducked below the fence.

Rory was moving around the far side of the corral. He stopped at the corner and waited for a moment for any sound. Hearing nothing, he peeked around the corner. It was clear. About ten feet to his left was another corral.

Rory started to walk between them, looking both ways, waiting for a gunman to reveal himself.

Minutes before, Cal had moved from the first corral to the next. He knelt at the back corner, watching Rory stand up and walk between the two corrals. Cal quickly advanced to the back edge and peeked around. Rory's back was to him. Staying close to the fence line, Cal stood and slowly followed Rory for a few feet, then stopped and aimed. Just as he was about to squeeze the trigger, the boom of a heavy rifle sounded. It was the sound of a Sharps 45-70 buffalo rifle. The force of the impact lifted Cal off his feet. When Rory turned, the sight he witnessed was Cal in the air, his back slamming onto the ground… Dead.

Neither Duke nor Jacob realized what had just happened. The boom of the big rifle echoed off the barn, causing both men to jump unexpectedly. They, however, weren't the only ones. It also spooked the cattle, bunching them up into the opposite corner. In doing so, it left an opening that both Jacob and Duke realized simultaneously, and at that exact moment, they fired through the fencing.

"You snake?" Duke yelled out.

Jacob ran to the corner of the corral. Looking around, he saw Duke lying on the ground, his gun a few feet away from him. He was clutching his belly, his shirt and hand covered with blood. Jacob approached him; blood oozed from his lips. He didn't speak. The hate and anger in his eyes told Jacob what he couldn't say.

Looking down at the outlaw, Jacob said, "Who's got the bellyache now?"

Duke turned his head and stretched out his arm. His fingers stretched, trying to reach for his gun. Determined for revenge right up to the end.

Elmer, the owner of the Livery, came running over with his Sharps rifle in hand. "You fellas all right? Who's this?" he said, looking down at the dead gunman.

"No one anymore," Jacob announced.

Rory walked up from behind Elmer. "Tat must have been ye who saved my hide."

"Sure was," said Elmer. "Me and my ol' Betsy, you bet. She's a trustworthy soul, the only one I can bet on to get me out of a scrape."

"I, for one, am mighty glad for yer help, Elmer," Rory said. "Can ye round up some lads to take care of these outlaws, my friend?

"You bet, I can."

While he's doing that," Jacob said. "We should check on the sheriff, then ask to check his wanted posters. I'd bet there's a wanted poster on one of these two. If so, the reward is yours, Elmer, for coming to our rescue."

"Why, that's mighty nice of ya fellas. Now, don't ya worry none. I'll get the wagon and a few men, and this trash will be cleaned up in no time."

Rory patted Elmer on the back and followed Jacob outside. When they stepped onto the main street, they saw men milling around. A few of them were on the roof of the boardwalk. With their boots, they pushed the hired gun off, and his body landed on the dirt street, kicking up dust around it.

Robert, the mercantile owner, came over when he spotted the two. "What about the others?" he asked.

"Elmer's gettin' a wee wagon hooked up to load 'em up. He might be needin' a bit o' help, you see." Rory said.

Robert hollered at some men, shuffling around. "You men go help Elmer at the livery."

"How's the sheriff?" Jacob asked.

"We took him over to Doc's office. He has a bullet in his right shoulder that needs to be removed, and the other went through his side. Doc said it looked clean. He'll patch them up, but it might be a few weeks before he's back on duty."

"Glad he's alive," Rory said, thanking Robert before he left to order others around. Rory smirked and shook his head, breathing hard. "Frank Wettin… he's done with this dust bowl. He deserves nothin' bet'er than a dirt blanket."

Rory checked his Colt and holstered it, glancing at Jacob. "Tucson, huh? Looks like we ain't done ridin' yet."

The two men headed for their horses. "Discovered at the land office that Wettin filed a false claim, the wee scoundrel! The location he filed was far from my land outside the Pioneer Mining District. So, I went ahead and filed the proper one. How about that, Aye? Now, let's get those deeds sorted out in Tucson."

The two men swung their legs over the saddles, turned their horses down Main Street, Florence, and headed south to Tucson.

Several hours later, the Arizona wind carried away the echoes of gunfire and chaos from the dusty streets of Florence, leaving the town quiet once more.

Chapter Eighteen

RORY AND JACOB RODE their horses at an easy gallop, taking frequent rest breaks. Their horses were fit and well-adapted to the trails, capable of completing the 70-mile journey in eight to ten hours. However, they wanted to ensure the horses were in good condition when they reached Tucson. The next morning they crossed the Rillito River. A few miles ahead, they could see the brick and adobe buildings and the hastily constructed adobe homes scattered throughout the valley. The heat of the day began early. As a whirlwind kicked up around them, they guided their horses down Stone Street, with the territorial capital now only a few streets away.

Rory had been here before. When they dismounted and wrapped the reins around the hitching post, they couldn't help but notice the crowd of people and wagons around the crude adobe structure housing the capital. "I was expecting more," Jacob said.

"How do you mean?" Rory questioned.

"The Capitol building?" Jacob nodded toward it. Several covered wagons stood out front as people rushed in and out of the building. "You weren't just a kidding when ya said they were moving to Phoenix soon. Looks like today, I was expectin' somethin' more… grand… my family's chicken coops were in better shape." As they stepped onto the wooden boardwalk in front of the sheriff's office, he added, "At least the sheriff's got himself a fine place." With a grin, he tipped his hat to Rory and tapped on the door as a warning that someone was coming in. He turned the doorknob and pushed the door open, it creaked, echoing like a pair of swinging batwing doors on an old saloon, never oiled.

The two stepped into the office.

"Howdy, men," the sheriff said as he stood from the chair behind his desk. "I'm Sheriff Virgil Deerborn; what can I do for ya today?"

"Sheriff, I'm Rory McDuncan; I ranch south of the mining town of Pinal. This is my friend Jacob Long." They shook the sheriff's hand.

"Yes, yes. Been expecting you. Got your telegram right here—just give me a moment to dig it out from this heap of papers on my desk," he drawled, riffling through the clutter with a knowing grin. "Ah, here it is. Took care of it first thing, y'know. Mighty convenient havin' the telegram office and the capital building right next door, wouldn't ya reckon?" He stood tall, hands propped on his hips, a broad smile plastered across his weathered face.

"So, did ye arrest Wettin?" Rory asked.

"No, sir. Reckon, he wandered into the capital office right after I took my leave. The clerk mosied on over to me later, saying the fella was fixin' to file some deeds. But as soon as the clerk laid eyes on his name, he shook his head and told him all transactions were on hold. Said he'd best have a word with the sheriff first if he wanted to get things moving."

"Let me guess," said Jacob. "He never showed."

"Right, ye are, young man. So, I took myself over to the Hotel and found out he and his man high-tailed it out of town right after."

"Any idea at all where he's goin'? Although I'd reckon he's headin' back to his ranch, says I," Rory speculated.

"But there's more to the tale," the sheriff drawled on, pushing his hat up with his finger. "After that, I strolled on over to the livery. The owner, ol' Horace, he tells me that this Frank and his hired man had come by to fetch the horses. But they wasn't riding solo. No, sir—he'd picked up some new companions. Six of 'em, to be particular. They all rode off together, a right motley crew. Horace, bein' the curious sort, stood watch from the livery entrance and saw them take the southeast trail instead of heading south toward Florence. Thought it mighty strange at first."

"Hired guns," Jacob said.

"Yup, you can always spot the folks itchin' for a scrap or hopin' to cash in easy. It's like a brand on their foreheads, clear as day in the dusty light of the saloon."

"Couldn't hae said it better ma'self," Rory said.

"Sheriff, what's southeast of here?" Jacob asked.

"Well now, partner, not much more to spin. Headin' south, you'll find yerself takin' a trail that climbs up into them rugged mountains, eventually leadin' ya to the mining camps of Globe. The only real spread worth mentioning along that dusty road is the Mason Ranch, which lies between that trail an' Florence. Those folks there are tough as nails, and their cattle? They're the finest around. Ain't no doubt about that."

"He's taken' the longer but less traveled road," Rory said.

"Sheriff, do ya know if the Territorial Marshal had an arrest warrant made out for Frank Wettin?" Jacob asked.

"I reckon he did; however, he aimed to have a word with some other ranchers 'fore he started makin' any arrests. He ought to be ridin' into the mining district in a few days. Had a bit of a situation to tend to further west first."

"Much obliged for your help, Sheriff," Jacob said and shook his hand.

Rory did the same. The men stepped out of the office. "Aye, think we'll be gettin' some grub from one o' the local cafés here 'fore we head fer home."

"Well, I'll tell ya," Sheriff Virgil pointed at the signs a few blocks west. Most of the cafés are Mexican with some of the best sopapillas, chiles, and beans in the territory. Mama's Café and Bakery is a few more blocks west. Best beef stew around, and the baked goods are made fresh daily."

Rory looked at Jacob and said, "Aye, don't know about ye, lad, but fresh loaf and buttery biscuits with a hearty stew sound absolutely grand!"

"Mama's it is then. Thanks for the suggestions," Jacob said. They unhitched the reins from the post and saddled up.

An hour later, their stomachs filled, they stepped onto the street when a wagon pulled by a team of horses kicking up dust passed by. Suddenly, the driver yelled,

"Woo!" and pulled back hard on the reins. The wagon abruptly stopped as the dust caught up to it. When the dust settled, the man on the wagon was staring back at them. "Well, I'll be if it isn't that o' Irish coot. 'Bout didn't recognize you without that big o' red beard," he said with a big smile.

"Rory leaned forward; Ed, you crazy o' prospector, is that you?"

Ed climbed down and walked to the wagon's back edge. Rory and Jacob walked over and shook his hand. "Ed Schieffelin what a surprise. Made it back to ye mine, did you? Did ye find that los' brother Albert of yours, did ye?"

"Sure did, at the McCracken Mine up north. Also got me an assayer as a partner, a name of Richard Gird. Offered him a grubstake, and he took it." Ed pulled back the tarp on the wagon. "Running my first load of silver ore for the stamper and smelter. Got two silver strikes. Call one the Lucky Cuss and the other the Tough Nut. He says the mines should produce $15,000 a ton. Should bring fifteen to twenty thousand dollars. But don't tell anyone. Got enough prospectors down around Bisbee and the Tombstone camp.

"Ed, I'd like you to meet a good friend, Jacob Long." The two men shook hands.

"Any friend of Rory is a friend of mine. Yes, sir."

"Ed came tae work for me in '77 as a temporary hired hand, he did. He drifted over to the Silver King Mine, hopin' to find his brother Al, but lo and behold, he found out the lad had moved on some 300 miles further northwest, so he did."

"Right, the McCracken Mine," Jacob said.

"That's right. I was completely broke. Spent my last 30 cents on tobacco," Ed said. "Figured if'n I was gonna die of starvation, I'd do it in comfort, yes siree. Well, now, let me spin ya a yarn here Jacob, by boy. Rory here… he's a good soul, supplin' up at the mercantile while I was busy parting with my last coin. Out of the blue, he hears me talking to the clerk, he steps up and offers me a job. I reckon I owe him a heap of gratitude for that. He let me toil away until I scraped together enough to gather supplies and get my mule shod proper-like. Ain't that the way of good folks in this wild frontier?

"Now that's a tale to remember," Jacob said.

"Ed, did I hear you call your camp the Tombstone?" Rory asked.

"Sure did. Couldn't help it. Seems to fit."

"Funny thing," Rory said to Jacob. "Ed once told me that a soldier mate warned him, 'If ye keep gallivantin' across the highlands in search of gold an' silver with the locals, the only stone ye'll be findin' will be yer own tombstone restin' beneath the heather.'"

"Came a tad close, that's for certain… but I ain't quite there yet," Ed drawled, squinting against the sun. "I've got a load to haul that needs tendin'. Mighty good to see ya again, Rory. And Jacob, if'n ya find yourself wanderin' 'round my neck of the woods and need anythin', toss my name 'round. Someone'll know me indeed."

<hr>

As the sun set on the dusty trail, Rory and Jacob knew it was time to stop for the night. They were half way in to thier ride back to Florence. Their horses had little downtime in Tucson and needed rest, food, and water. The two weary travelers themselves could use a break from the long journey.

They found a suitable spot near a creek in the shallow arroyo, surrounded by rocks and trees. The massive cottonwood trees help give them cover. After starting a small cookfire, they put the coffee on first. While sipping hot coffee, they added salt pork to the skillet to fry. Next, Jacob added some chopped potatoes, onions, and a little lard and water mixed with the meat's juices to sauté the potatoes and onions. When everything was finished, they took a couple of slices of fresh bread they bought at Mama's café and served their skillet meal on top. After cleaning up, they set up their bedrolls and settled in for the night. As darkness fell, the silence of the desert was broken only by the crackling of the fire and coyotes in the distant hills.

Little did they know that three highwaymen, notorious outlaws who often robbed the local stagecoaches, had been watching their every move from a distance. They saw the flickering flames of the campfire and assumed it was an easy target for robbing. Creeping closer, they planned to take their victims by surprise.

But Jacob, always alert and cautious, had positioned himself in the wooded area along the creek, hidden from view. Rory was sleeping against a large cottonwood a few feet from the fire. As the outlaws approached the campfire, Jacob quietly emerged from the shadows and confronted them. "Drop your guns, boys, and reach for the stars."

The outlaws were taken aback by Jacob's sudden appearance, but they quickly regained their composure and turned to fire their weapons. Shots rang out in the dark, and chaos erupted as the men stumbled and dodged among the rocks, trees, and brush. Rory quickly retrieved his rifle and moved around the tree for cover.

The outlaws were confident they had the upper hand but didn't anticipate their adversaries' experience and quick reflexes. They were adept with their guns and understood how to utilize the terrain to their advantage. Rory stepped further into the trees, keeping his eyes on the open areas around the fire. The light from the fire would give him an advantage if a gunman passed through the area. He knew Jacob would not allow himself to come into the light where he could easily be seen by the outlaws.

Jacob moved like a cat, each step silently navigating around brush and over twigs. He kept his gaze away from the campfire, something the enemy had failed to do. Leaning against a tree, he waited patiently. The footsteps on soil and twigs grew louder. Just a few feet away, a gunman stepped into the clearing, unaware of Jacob's presence.

"I gave you a chance," Jacob said. "Drop it or die."

The outlaw turned and fired, but his bullet struck a tree a few feet away—his vision still adjusting from the brightness of the firelight. Jacob's shot, on the other hand, was true and effective.

The sharp crack of a rifle echoed through the clearing; the sturdy piece of craftsmanship, with a polished wooden stock, was propped firmly against the rough bark of the oak tree, providing vital support and the precision needed for a clean shot. One of the outlaws—a lanky figure clad in tattered leather and a wide-brimmed hat—darted past the flickering campfire. He believed that by rushing toward the source of the sound, he could outmaneuver the shooter or assist his comrade in peril. However, in his haste and folly, he was gravely mistaken.

Moments later, all fell silent. Even the crickets hushed. The only sound that could be heard was the hoofbeats of a horse fading into the night.

Chapter Nineteen

As the sun began to set, it cast warm orange glow rings around the clouds and onto the mountains to the east. Rory McDuncan and Jacob Long halted their horses at the edge of the McDuncan Ranch. It felt strange for Rory to camp on his land, just thirty minutes away from the ranch, but with night approaching, they chose caution and set up camp rather than risk riding into the ranch in the dark.

Selecting a small clearing nestled between two ancient oak trees in an arroyo would offer shelter from the chilly evening breeze. The familiar scents of earth and wildflowers put the men at ease. Rory struck the wooden match, adding flame to the tinder Jacob brought for the fire. Shortly, the warmth of a crackling fire dispelled the cool air as they prepared their cookfire meal. They took turns keeping watch throughout the night until they began their final journey home in the morning.

Alisa was finishing up straightening her bed, the sun filtering through her window casting warm patches of light across the room. She caught movement out of the second-story window as she tossed the last pillow into place and slipped on her dress. Her heart skipped a beat as she spotted two familiar riders approaching, their figures silhouetted against the bright sky. Excitedly, she dashed down the staircase, her voice echoing through the house as she called out, "They're back!"

Sophia emerged from the kitchen, wiping her hands on a dish towel, a smudge of flour dusting her brow. She looked up, curiosity in her eyes, as Alisa hurriedly shared the news. The two rushed onto the porch, standing side by side in anticipation and relief as they watched the riders draw closer. The horses' hooves thudded softly against the gravel path as they rode around the corral to the barn.

Alisa jumped off the porch and ran to the barn. Jacob had handed the reins to Cali when Alisa leaped into Jacob's arms. She wrapped her arms around him and held him close. He had not felt such devotion since childhood in his own mother's embrace.

"I missed you so," she said, looking up with a tear.

"We were gone less then a week," he remarked.

"Doesn't matter. I still missed you. Mother and I were worried. We prayed every day for you and Father, for your safe return."

"I'm much obliged that you would do that for me. It seems our adventures were watched over by you and the good Lord above.

After dinner, they all sat around the table. Jacob and Cali helped clear the table so the ladies could join in on their discussion. "Before we left Tucson, the sheriff informed us that Wettin had ridden off with six other men," Jacob said as he sat down at the table.

"Gunmen," said Rory in frustration. "Aye, he's plannin' on causin' more harm; I just know it."

"That might explain the heavy black smoke we saw to the north. We didn't dare ride over to help if the ranch was attacked. There wouldn't have been anyone here but the women to defend it," Henry said.

"Heavy black smoke would mean a structure's burnin', I'd say. 'As much as I'd love to sit this one out, I know well enough that Wettin will never call it quits, so he won't." Rory said.

"We've got to get the word out, and the sheriff needs to know. We also need to find out if the Marshall is in the area. I want to take Cali and head into Pinal, if'n ya don't mind Rory?"

"No, not at all, lad. Four days on the trail and my ol' bones are achin' something fierce. I'll just sit on the porch rocker a spell with m' rifle in me lap."

Alisa didn't want him to leave and told him so. She knew, however, that someone had to stand against injustice and help their neighbors. "I need you to be careful. If something were to happen to you, I'd never find another Jacob Long."

"Well, I wouldn't mind if you kept praying for me. My mother always told me there's power in prayer, and I'm starting to realize she was right." Jacob gave her a kiss, climbed onto the saddle, tipped his hat to her, and rode off with Cali following.

It was nearly noon by the time Cali and Jacob rode into town. Their first stop was Sheriff Leroy Payne. Cali stayed on the boardwalk as Jacob stepped into the sheriff's office. "Well, I'll be! Look who we have here. After a week, I suspected you were rotting somewhere in the desert, coyotes gnawing on ya. But I'm glad you're alive. Didn't want to have to drag your bones back here with coyotes attached for a dirt nap."

Jacob shook his hand. "Mighty glad you think so highly of me," he said with a grin. "Heard there was a fire. Any details?"

Evans Place got bunted out. Somehow, some of the livestock got caught in the barn as it went up. There's nothing left of it. They lost everything except the house and a few horses. Guess who showed up while the barn was still smoldering?"

"Wettin."

"That's right. Right, along with more hired guns. Evans and some of the other ranchers are ready to form a vigilante gang against Wettin. But I think they're still too scared since he has more men now."

"That's why I'm here," Jacob said. "He hired six more gunmen in Tucson. I was hoping the marshal was around. We need to put a stop to it before it gets more out of hand."

"Your lucky day. Right now, he's up at the Silver King Mine inquiring about the mine on Mr. McDuncan's land… pulled out early this mornin'. Said he'd be back sometime after the noon hour."

"I'm thinkin' we put a posse together for tomorrow mornin'. Get a jump on Wettin before he stirs up any more trouble."

"That's good by me. The marshal's got the arrest warrant. I'm sure he'd appreciate the help. Why don't you cover the saloons? See if ya can round up any volunteers. Tell them I'll pin a badge on them and pay twenty dollars a day. That should drum up some business."

"Sounds mighty fine. Can the town afford that?"

"Ya kidding. With as much silver and gold dust changing hands, the city fathers collect land rent, of which twenty percent goes back into the town's general fund to pay for my services, burials, and civic services. It's a pretty big pot."

The sheriff stepped behind his desk and pulled three badges from a drawer. "Got ten of these things," he said, holding up the badges. "City founders knew that where there's boomtowns, there's theft and murder. They wanted to be prepared for the day they needed more lawmen."

"Good foresight on their part," Jacob commented.

"Cali, step in here," the sheriff called out. Cali stepped into the office. "Now, don't tell the marshal Rory wasn't here. I am deputizing you both, and Rory even if he's not here, in the name of the law. Duly recognized by an official of the law until such matters are completed. Jacob, this badge is a Deputy Marshal's badge for the territory of Arizona. By doing this, someone will still have the authority if something happens to me, you, or the marshal. The other two are for Cali and Rory," handing the two badges to Cali.

Jacob and Cali put the badges into their pockets and headed for the Bottomers Saloon first. Cali stayed outside again, keeping watch. Both Monte and Ricky were behind the bar, cleaning glasses. "Jacob, step on up; drinks are on me," Monte waved him over.

No, just a coffee if you've some made."

"I do, be right back." Monte set the coffee cup on the bar counter. "I've heard rumors of trouble and discussions in the saloon while serving drinks. So, what can I help with?"

"I've been deputized, Monte." Monte was quiet and picked up a whiskey glass to clean. "I'm hunting up paid volunteers." Jacob's voice got louder as he turned away from the bar. "The Territorial Marshal has an arrest warrant. Any man worth his salt who is willing to volunteer will be deputized and receive a pay of twenty dollars a day. If you or someone you know is willing to volunteer, please meet at the sheriff's office no later than sunup tomorrow morning."

Jacob turned back to Monte with a grin. "Do you think I'll have any takers?"

"I believe, if'n they're willing to pretend to be sick and not show up for work, they could earn about a week's wages in a day. You'll get some interest."

"Great, thanks for the coffee, Monte. Feel free to share the information. I'll be doing the same at the other saloons in town."

Sheriff Payne met Jacob and Cali walking down the boardwalk, returning from the last saloon. Payne had the Territory Marshal with him. "I'd like you to meet Marshal Lee Colter. Marshal, this is the man I've told you about, Jacob Long." The two shook hands. "And this is Cali; he's a fine hired hand of the McDuncan Ranch. "The marshal shook Cali's hand. "Glad to meet you, son." Cali smiled. "*Sí señor, gracias.*"

"Well, gentlemen. I'm hungry. Did I tell you that as deputies, you have an expense account that includes the finest steaks at the Corner Café?"

"Well, since you're buying the heifer, I'm in. Come on, Cali," Jacob said. "The food always tastes better when someone else is buying."

Seven men rode into the desolate landscape of the Evans Ranch, their silhouettes stark against the early evening sky. To the east lay the Pinal Mountains, and to the north, the majestic Superstitions. The once vibrant ranch now lay in ruins, with only the modest adobe home of Jake and Mariam Evans standing amidst the charred remnants. The barn and corrals flickered with dying embers, still smoldering from the fierce blaze that had consumed them two days prior. The couple, who had once nurtured dreams of a thriving ranch filled with children's laughter, now faced an unforgiving reality; their hopes had been reduced to ashes, along with most of their prized breeding stock lost in the disastrous fire.

Devastation hung heavy in the air, as the weight of their loss pressed down on their shoulders. Frank Wettin rode in at the end of the day when the flames had left nothing but blackened timbers. With a feigned expression of sympathy, he offered his condolences and gave them 48 hours to relinquish the deed to their land. His offer was a paltry sum—only fifty cents on the dollar of its true value, a fraction of the amount he had proposed just months earlier. The true value of the land was the small creek that flowed through it, a steady stream of spring water seeping from the earth somewhere in the mountains to the north. The shadows of despair and betrayal deepened around Jake and Mariam as they struggled with their loss and the presence of a man who, for some unknown reason, sought to profit from their tragedy.

Two days later, Jake met the men on horseback at the door, holding a double-barrel shotgun while his wife stood behind him just inside the threshold.

"I gave you 48 hours, Mr. Evans. Your time is up. What will it be?" Frank Wettin announced in a stern voice.

"I have no mind to part with my land, not for such a paltry sum. Your first offer was a mere pittance, far beneath what this land is truly worth," Evans fired back.

"I'll tell you what—Mr. Evans and Mrs. Evans. I'm a fair man. I'll give you the original offer. You can make a fresh start somewhere with a more suitable climate, like California. The weather's always nice, and there are a lot more people you could sell your horses to… by golly, I'm feeling generous! I'll even throw in a wagon and tack since you lost yours in the fire. I'm sure you've still got some horses to pull it," he said as he looked around at his men, "Heck, my boys will even help you pack. The good news is you'll be getting away from this tinder box. I would hate to see your modest home have the same consequences as your barn. The loss of your belongings and memories reduced to nothing but ash." Wettin just sat on his horse, leaning on the pommel horn with a smug look.

Jake looked back at his wife in the doorway. Her expression of their possible loss was evident on her face. Jake turned back to Wettin. "We'll consider it, Mr. Wettin. But please give us another day to discuss what to do, and where to go."

"I'll give until sundown. I'll be back with the wagon in tow. Have the deed ready. I won't have any more conversations." Wettin turned and rode off; his gunmen followed.

"Mariam, I am so sorry for all this. I'm positive it was Wettin and his men who burnt down our barn."

"It's not your fault, Jake. Men like that care nothing for others, only their evil ways."

"I need to ride in and tell the sheriff. The marshal is 'spose to be in the area. If they don't have a plan or are unwilling to help, we'll take the deal and move on. Agreed?" Mariam shook her head in agreement.

Jake stepped out the back door where he kept his saddle horses, with Mariam following closely behind. He removed the saddle from the hitching rail, quickly saddled his horse, and climbed on. "I'll be back as soon as I can. Stay inside and keep the shotgun and pistol handy. I'm sure they won't bother us until tonight," Jake turned his horse into a run. Staying off the road toward town.

Chapter Twenty

THE FOUR MEN SAT in the café, visiting and hashing out a plan for arresting Wettin. "I've talked with the mine supervisor about the mine on your property. He sent a couple of inspectors and an assayer to the location and spoke with your crew. The inspectors got the full story from the miners and the kidnapping. That alone will put him away for fifteen years. I had the inspectors sign an affidavit, which helped make the warrant more lawful. If everything else you tell me can be verified, he'll get put away for a long time."

"We'll just have to talk to a few more ranchers then," said Sheriff Payne.

Jacob interrupted. "Might not have to," he said, glaring out the café window, "Evans just rode up with a trail of dust behind him." All turned and looked through the window and immediately headed for the door. As the men crossed the street, Jake Evans came out of the sheriff's office.

"Thank God you're all here. I got worried when the office was empty."

"What's the problem, Evans?" the sheriff asked.

"Frank Wettin rode into the ranch with six hired guns on the very day of the fire. He offered me cash for my land, but I had no interest in sellin'. No, sir, I had no mind to give it up. Still, he wouldn't take no for an answer, giving me 48 hours to ponder it. He rode in today with his men. This time, he came with a smaller offer, half of what he'd promised before. When I stood my ground and told him I wasn't interested, he changed his tune again, offering the original amount then sweetening the deal with a wagon to help us pack up our lives and start fresh in California."

"And, what was his response to that?" the marshal asked.

"He warned us, plain as day, that if we turned down his deal, we'd likely lose our homestead to another fire, just like the one that had already taken our barn and corral. He's given us 'til sundown to make our choice. I can't lay my hands on proof, but I know in my bones it was he who set our barn ablaze. If I refuse his offer, I'm dead certain he'll see to it that we're burned out for good."

"An' I'm dead certain he'll do it tonight," Jacob said angrily.

"Ar'ya men in for an all-night stakeout?" the marshal asked. All agreed.

"Cali, you've got the best horse. Ride back to the ranch and bring Rory with you. Explain what we're planning tonight and let him know we're organizing a pose in the morning. Let the womenfolk know it could be a few days. Bring our overnight gear and stay off the trails and main road—out of sight of the Evans Ranch."

"That's a good plan," the sheriff said. Cali, meet us in the wooded area along the hills to the east. We'll stay out of sight until night. Under the cover of darkness, we'll move into place and wait."

Cali shook his head slowly, a man of few words. He took up the reins to his horse and leaped on. Put his finger to his hat and tipped it. "*Adios!*" His actions often conveyed his thoughts. With a rugged charm and an unmistakable presence, he was the finest hired hand the McDuncan Ranch has ever had. His rich Mexican heritage infused him with a deep-rooted connection to the land, and his unmatched skills made him the best choice to accompany Rory to the Evans Ranch.

Unsure how many men would be in the posse, Marshal Lee, Sheriff Payne, and Deputy Marshal Long secured a pack horse from the livery and gathered extra ammunition from the sheriff's office and three days' worth of food from the mercantile store. They planned to secure the Evans Ranch throughout the night. Sheriff Payne would return to town before sunrise to assemble the posse. They would meet at the Evans Ranch and wait for Rory and Cali. Once everyone arrived, they would take the northwest trail to the Four Peaks Ranch to arrest Frank Wettin.

It took the three lawmen and Jake Evans less than an hour to reach his ranch. Jake felt a wave of relief when he saw that his home was still standing. As they led their horses to the back of the house, out of sight of the trail, Mrs. Evans came out to greet them. In her mid-twenties, Mariam had grown up on a horse ranch, acquiring extensive knowledge of horses. Often surpassing her husband in skills, she managed both equine and household responsibilities effectively. Her husband, Jake, was only a few years older than Mariam. He had worked as a cowboy for some of the largest cattle ranches in Texas until he met Mariam, and together they established their life in Arizona.

Mariam embraced her husband with a long hug when he dismounted, clearly relieved that he was safely back.

"Mariam, this is Marshal Lee and Jacob Long, and you know Sheriff Payne," Jake introduced his fellow lawmen.

She held her hand up to shade her eyes. "Pleased to meet you, gentlemen and sheriff; good to see you again.

"Have you men had your breakfast this morning?" Mrs. Evans asked.

"Yes, ma'am, we have," Marshal Lee replied.

"Mariam," Sheriff Payne said. "I have a question. We plan to set up a camp in the treeline on the east ridge until it gets dark, then move here, around the house, after dark. We are concerned for your safety tonight. Would you be willing to stay at our camp away from the house tonight?"

"Sheriff Payne, Leroy, you're a good man, and I appreciate all your concerns. However, I would feel just as safe inside my home as I would outside. It is a sturdy, well-built home. It would take a lot to burn this place down. I will stay here tonight."

"Yes, ma'am," the sheriff replied.

Marshall Lee stepped forward, a steely glint in his eye. "Listen here, Jake. Your job then is to keep yer homestead safe from any no-good scoundrels tryin' to break through that door. Make sure ya stock up on water and blankets; if that fire gets inside, you'll be needin' 'em. When the sun sets, we'll spread out 'mongst the trees, coverin' all sides.

When Wettin and his gang come ridin' in, we'll be ready for 'em.

"I can do that. What'll I do when Wettin gets here?"

"Politely turn down his offer. Tell him you've mulled it over and you're fixin' to stay put. If he starts gettin' pushy, stand your ground. Firmly tell him you ain't runnin' and you sure as shootin' ain't givin' up. A man like him only understands strength and determination. But remember, do all this from behind your doorstep. Don't give 'em an open target. If it comes to it, you point that rifle right at him and tell him to get off your land. We'll be watchin' your back, partner. You got it?" The marshal put a comforting hand on Jake's shoulder.

Jake looked at Mariam, and she shook her head. He turned back to the marshal, "We understand. We can do it."

"Now, all you men, listen to me," Mariam announced. "I have a big pot of stew and dumplings cooking with canned peaches and fresh bread in the oven. I expect you back here at noon for lunch. No exceptions. Now I'll leave you men to do what you need to do." No one had a chance to say otherwise. She turned on a heel and returned to the house.

"After all that, I don't think renegade Apaches or a gunfight with outlaws could keep me away from that stew," Jacob said.

"They laughed as they mounted and turned their horses toward the east ridge line."

Rory and Cali rode in about mid-afternoon. They rode through the hills, staying off the main roads and trails. Mariam gave Sheriff Payne the leftover stew and bread for Rory and Cali. It was on the fire coals keeping warm. Thankful for their meal, the two cleaned the pot and finished the bread.

"*Señor* Payne. Please, thank *Señorita* Evans for me. The stew and bread were good," Cali said.

"And thank her for me, Aye," Rory added.

Two hours before sundown, the posse spread out just in time. A dust cloud appeared on the road as seven riders approached quickly. Their goal was to show force in hopes of intimidating the Evans. They rode fast and stopped just as fast with the dust pushing past them.

"Evans! Jake Evans!" Wettin shouted. "I'm here for your decision."

The door opened slowly. Jake revealed just enough of himself, keeping his rifle out of sight. "What do you want, Wettin?" he called back.

There was a moment of confusion before Wettin responded. "You know very well what I want. Do you have your deed ready?"

"No, I do not," Jake replied firmly. "I am not selling my land, not to you or anyone else. We have discussed our options and are staying put. There's nothing left to discuss. Take your men and ride out."

"Wettin's tone turned serious. "Evans, that is not what I wanted to hear. You have no options, no choices, and by tomorrow, you may have no home. Am I making myself perfectly clear?"

"Wettin, I'm afraid not. Now let me make myself perfectly clear," Jake put his rifle up against the door jam for a steady shot. "I don't take kindly to trespassers. Now, get off my land or this here Sharps will shoot you right off your saddle and take with you a few of them hired guns lined up behind you." The outlaws looked at each other and backed their ponies away.

Wettin looked around at his men moving back. Without another word, he turned his horse and gigged it into a run. The hired guns followed.

It was dark under a waxing moon. Having experience with renegades and outlaws, Marshal Lee knew they would wait until the lights were out and their targets would be asleep. The men slept, taking turns at watch.

It was eleven in the evening when the lanterns were extinguished. Two hours later, the men moved into new positions. With his Yellow Boy, a model 1866 Henry rifle known for its yellowish brass receiver, Rory moved further up the tree line, giving him a clear view of the area from the trail to the house. His job was to protect their backs and eliminate anyone attempting to enter the back of the house, if possible.

Cali, the youngest and most observant member of the group, had cat-like eyes that adapted perfectly to the darkness. Positioned on the rooftop, he could detect movements that others missed. Agile and quick, he handled his rifle with expert precision, ready to defend his comrades from any threats lurking in the night. If a torch made it to the top of the house, he could get to it.

The others spread out around the ranch. Marshal Lee took his position behind the scorched wagon next to the barn. Further away from the barn, Sheriff Payne climbed a haystack that covered the middle of the ranch yard. He lay on top of the hay pile, his rifle covering the far end of the ranch yard. Jacob waited under the porch, giving him a clear view of the road.

They waited so long that they began to think Marshal Lee was wrong and began to doze off. Three hours passed when the galloping of hoofs was heard. The men came out of their slumber wide-eyed and ready. Through the trees along the trail, torches of fire could be seen. The outlaws all emerged from the dirt road, their horses at a full run, then split up when they entered the ranch yard. It was as if they knew the lawmen were there, making it difficult to put a bead on them. The sound of the first rifle came from behind the house. The only thing Rory could see from his cover was the torch and the arm of the rider. He fired at the torch, knocking it out of the rider's hand. Just as that happened, a torch flew through the air, nearly hitting Cali. It was so close that he could pick it up and throw it into the yard behind the house.

Hearing the rifle shot, the outlaws scattered even more, making their runs at the house. They assumed it was the homeowners shooting from the house. A rider came around the burnt-out barn and wagon, crossed by Marshal Lee without seeing him, and headed for the house. Lee aimed and knocked the outlaw off his horse. As the horse ran past the front of the house, another rider rode by and threw a torch through a window. A rifle shot came from the window but missed the rider. In his escape, that rider headed for the far end of the ranch yard, lining up in Sheriff Payne's sights; he waited until the rider silhouetted against the fire from the house and dropped the outlaw with a single shot. The remaining riders realized it was an ambush, hollering to the others, "It's an ambush, let's get out of here," and headed for the road. Cali and Jacob took a few wild shots but were unsure if they had hit any outlaws.

The lawmen were victorious but waited. Rushing out in the open could be the difference between life and death if an outlaw or two set an ambush after their retreat. It wasn't long before Rory came riding up the road to the ranch yard. "It's Rory," he called out to the ranch, stopped his horse, and waited for a reply.

"Come on in, Rory," The sheriff yelled.

The other men came out from their cover, but Cali stayed on the roof of the house as a lookout. He was always one step ahead regarding their safety. "Rory, what are ya doing on the road?" the marshal asked.

"Made my way through the woods fer about a mile, then waited. By the sounds o' it, I reckoned ye had things well in hand. Just before long, a bunch o' four riders came racing by. I wasn't sure how many there were, so I doubled back on the other side of the road, just in case any had stayed behind. But I didn't find a soul."

"Thanks for taking the risk," the marshal said. My guess is six riders came in, but I'm not sure how many we got. I got one headin' for the house."

"I got one just after you did, Marshal, but I heard a shot behind the house." They all looked at Rory as he climbed down from his horse.

Aye, lad, that was me, alright. Aimed for the torch and smashed it out of his hand. That's all.

Jacob and Jake walked up to join them in the yard. "Sorry, we were out of it after the torch came through the window. I climbed out from cover and went inside to help the Evans put out the flames."

Might glad he did," said Jake. "That torch landed on the rug. We wrapped it up and hauled it out the back door."

"Reckon everyone's safe," the marshal said, tipping his hat slightly. "Ain't much we can do 'til the break of dawn. Let's check on the two we plugged and drag 'em over by the barn. We'll figure out who they are come morning. In the meantime, the sheriff and I will keep watch. Jake, could you rustle up some hot coffee from the Mrs? And Rory, why don't you, Cali, and Jacob head back to camp for a spell? Get some shuteye and stoke that cookfire for breakfast later on."

Jake headed back to the house while the others moved the bodies. When the other three headed for the campsite, the marshal and sheriff sat on the porch rocking chairs with rifles in their laps. While enjoying the rocking motion of the chair, the marshal turned to Sheriff Payne. "Well, now, I reckon that coffee would sure hit the spot right about now," he said as Mrs. Evans came out the door.

"One step ahead of you, Marshall. I already had it brewing on the stove," she said with a smile, handing them tin cups and pouring the anticipated steaming hot coffee.

Chapter Twenty-One

THE SUN WAS BEGINNING to rise, casting golden hues over the horizon, promising a day with unexpected challenges ahead. Sheriff Payne and Marshal Lee came into the campsite. "We've had some rest and already ate. I can throw on some chow for you," Jacob said.

"Nah, don't you worry 'bout that. Mrs. Evans done fed us right proper. I'll let y'all take the reins and lend a hand to the Evans with whatever needs doin'. Payne and me, we're lookin' to catch a few hours of shut-eye before we hit the trail again."

"Did ye get a chance to look at the two gunmen yet, Marshal?" Rory asked.

"Well, I did. Sorry, the noggin's a little cloudy. There's one feller I know fer sure. Got his mug on a wanted poster—name's Gunner Maverick. They're danglin' a thousand-dollar reward on his head for the murder of a lawman and for robbing some banks. Since it was me or Payne that put a bullet in him, we figured it'd be mighty kind to let the Evans collect that reward. That oughta be more than enough to build themselves a new barn and restock what they lost."

"Aye, that's a might nice thing to do for them. They're good folk, and they'll surely appreciate it!" Rory slapped the marshal on the back. "Well, lads, let's go see if Lee and Payne lef' a wee bit o' coffee for us, shall we?"

Two hours later, Marshal Lee approached the house. The door was open, and the glass and debris had been cleaned. The window was boarded, and the Evans were discussing how they could rebuild with the promised reward money. "Well, it looks like everything is under control."

"Good morning again, Marshal," Mariam said. "Did you get some rest?"

"Sure did, thank ya kindly, ma'am, and for coffee and breakfast. I'm feelin' a heap better now. But Sheriff Payne, well, he didn't rest. That man still had fight in him. he lit a shuck back to town before the break of dawn to rustle up a posse."

Jacob stood up from the table. "I reckon we should do the same."

"Like ya read my mind, son," the marshal said.

Rory stood up from the table, ready to leave. "Rory," Jacob said, "Cali and I will pack up the camp and our horses. If you take Cali's place and watch the yard, we'll bring the horses around. Jake, you and the Mrs. are on your own now. Hope you don't mind."

"Not at all, Jacob. The wife can shoot as well as I can. There's nothing left but the house, and if we run into any trouble, we can hold them off from here."

"Reckon it's good to hear. Once we clean up this whole mess, we'll rustle up a wagon for them outlaws. If'n ya like, ya can ride back t' town at the same time and collect on that reward." The Evans where excited and thanked them all.

Rory grabbed his rifle and headed out the door to relieve Cali. Jacob and the marshal exited through the back door. Thirty minutes later, they arrived in the ranch yard. Rory mounted his horse and waved at the Evans family, standing on the porch, before galloping out of the ranch and down the road.

"Sheriff Payne and the posse will meet us on the road, about a mile from Wettin's ranch," he said as he rode. No one spoke. They understood.

It took hours to reach what they estimated was a mile out, and then they worked their way into the tree line near the road. The marshal pulled out his pocket watch and said, "It's eight o'clock. I'm not sure if we're early or late. We need to scout the trail. Jacob, who would be the best person to scout out the Wettin ranch? We need to know how many we're up against."

Jacob looked at Cali. "You up to it?"

"*Sí,* I will."

"Find out as much as you can and report back in an hour," Jacob said.

"Good," the marshal replied, tipping his hat back slightly. He leaned onto his pommel horn. "Jacob, you ride with him in case we're in the wrong location. If'n ya run into the posse and they're settin' up in a good spot, you hustle back and let us know. If not, well, bring 'em on back here, ya hear?" Jacob nodded, then he and Cali set off down the road.

Still hidden from view of the sprawling Four Peaks Ranch, Cali left Jacob's side to find a vantage point for scouting. He ventured into the thick underbrush of an arroyo, his senses heightened as he navigated through the Desert Willow and Mesquite. Spotting the largest hill, he dismounted and tied his horse to an Ocotillo. Moving out of the wash, he began to climb the hill. As he slowly crested the top, he caught a glimpse of the ranch below him, its rustic charm standing out against the backdrop of the blue sky and rolling hills.

Jacob moved into the brush, but when he caught sight of the ranch, he turned and headed back. Upon returning to their location, he found Sheriff Leroy Payne and the deputized posse of only three extra men. Sheriff Payne rode over to him. "Sorry, that's all that showed."

"That gives us seven men. If we're not greatly outnumbered, we should be fine," Jacob remarked.

"All right, men, listen up! Dismount and rest 'til our scout returns," Marshal Lee commanded, his voice sounding as dry as a tumbleweed rolling through the dusty desert.

Rory dismounted, took his water sack, and handed it to the marshal. "Soundin' like an old heifer there, marshal. Why don't ye hang on to this one? Ah've got another!"

"Much obliged, I reckon I hurried off and forgot to refill mine."

"Aye, it happens to the best o' us."

It had been an hour, and there was still no sign of Cali. "You think he's alright?" Jacob asked Rory.

"Aye, nae bother. Instincts like a cat and just as many lives. When he gets hungry he'll return.

When Cali rode in, everyone stood to hear the news. Cali climbed down, the reins in his hands, and walked up to the three leaders. "Got any… *cecina para comer*… ah, Jerky to eat. Mine's gone.

Jacob looked at Rory, who in return gave him a wink. Jacob shrugged his shoulders and pulled a chunk out of his saddle bag and handed to Cali.

"What's the news, young man?" the marshal asked.

I watched for a long time. No outriders," he held up his fingers with the jerky as he spoke. "*Dos* men on the gate. *Dos* at the yard. *Uno en la casa, porche.* I wait. *Tres* go in and out el granero, barn. Maybe more in the bunkhouse."

"Well, that makes five like the hired hands said. Any sign of Wettin?" Rory asked.

"No, *Señor.* did not see him.

"Last time we were here, they had no one on watch at the gate or yard. So, they must be ready for something," Jacob said.

"We can still catch 'em off guard," the marshal said, his eyes narrowing with determination. "We'll circle 'round 'em, then I'll let out a holler to toss their weapons aside. To spare some lives, we'll let anyone who surrenders pass through without a scratch. Agreed?" They all nodded. "Alright, listen up. Sheriff, you take the posse and keep an eye on the rear and the sides. The rest of us will hold the front and the flanks. Remember, no shootin' less they shoot first. Got it?" They all nodded in agreement.

"Cali," Rory said, "Did ye scout a good place tae hide t' horses?"

"Sí, Señor. Sígame, por favor… follow me."

Moments later, the horses were in the arroyo, enjoying the cool water from a small stream and the grasses growing around it. They hobbled the horses, and the men moved to their assigned positions. The marshal emerged from behind a large tree near the gate and called out, "This is Arizona Territory Marshal Lee. The ranch is surrounded by a deputized posse!"

"What do you want, Marshal?" a hired gunman hollered from the gate.

"I have a warrant for the arrest of Frank Wettin. Tell him to come out and come along peacefully. Anyone willing to throw down their weapons can ride out with their life. If not, my deputies will shoot to kill." Marshall Lee ducked behind the tree just as one of the gate guards shot at him. None of the posse returned fire. "I will give you ten minutes to saddle up and ride out the front gate." No one responded. He waited.

Less than ten minutes passed when the gate was opened, allowing three men to pass through. They stopped when the marshal put out his hand. "Marshal, we're not gunmen. Just hired hands. We want nothing of this."

"I figured as much. How many hired guns are on the ranch?"

There are five left," one of the hired men said. Six went out early this morning. They woke me to bring the horses from the corral. But only four came back. We don't know the new men. Only Reed we know, he's one of the first hired. He got back a couple of days ago with Mr. Wettin."

"Where is Wettin now?"

"He's not here. He and his manager, Curby, rode out early this morning."

"Where's he ridin' to?"

"Sorry," the man shrugged. The marshal waved them on. The hired hands kicked their horses into a gallop.

Chapter Twenty-Two

THE SUN SET HIGH, casting very few shadows over the dusty landscape as he crouched low, weaving through the prickly brush. Every step, mindful of the possibility of rattlers hiding nearby. "It's the marshal, Rory," he called out, his voice steady despite the rustle of the dry leaves. "I'm comin' in."

"I see ye, come on over, will ye?" Rory said.

"Three hired hands gave it up and rode out the gate. Wanted nothing to do with the gunmen. I learned that Wettin ain't even at the ranch. He took off at first light with his man, Curby. Seems like the fella's got a nose for trouble—'spose he figured if we ambushed his men at the Evans place, we'd be heading his way too. You reckon you got any idea where those two might've skedaddled off to?" the marshal asked.

"I do, that weaseling skunk. Every bone in that man cries out with hate and revenge, it does. Marshal, Jacob and I need to be ridin' to m' ranch. I'm the only one who's bucked him all the way, I am! He'll be lookin' fer revenge and puttin' my womenfolk in danger."

"Alright, we'll hold down the rest of them here." As the marshal made his way back, the shooting began. Bullets whizzed by as he navigated back to his cover. The hired guns pulled a wagon in front of the gate for protection. "Give yourselves up," he shouted. "We have you outnumbered two to one," as a few bullets tore the bark off the tree he was using for cover.

Rory had to pull Jacob away from his cover as they made their way through the brush and cacti to where the horses were kept. They mounted up. "It's a long, hard ride. Are you up for it?" he asked Rory.

"Thanks for the concern; I'm still tougher than I look."

Jacob smiled. "Then let's ride," spurring their horses, they burst from their concealed location at a dead run.

Unaware of the posse flanking the property, the shooting began. One of the gate guards was hit. As he fell to the ground, the other was wounded in the leg. Dropping his rifle, he crawled under the wagon and leaned against the wheel. The remaining two hired guns hiding around a wagon near the barn didn't stand a chance. Outnumbered, there was nowhere for them to take cover except in the barn.

Reed was seated on the porch but moved inside when the shooting started, pressing against the door frame with his rifle in hand. He was unaware that someone had already infiltrated the ranch house. He raised his rifle against the door jamb as he watched the marshal emerge from behind the tree. He was about to pull the trigger. "Drop the rifle or I'll drop you. What'll it be?

Reed paused. "Okay, okay, don't shoot. I'll drop it. Reed turned slightly to the left and threw the rifle away from him. Hoping it would distract the posse member, he immediately reached for his pistol. Sheriff Payne was not fooled. Reed's gun barely cleared the holster before he dropped to the floor on his knees. Holding his chest, he gurgled with a smile, "Wasn't fast enough, eh?"

"No, wasn't smart enough," Sheriff Payne said just as Reed fell to the floor, dead.

Marshal Lee took advantage of the gunmen at the wagon and ran up to the gate before the wounded man could pull his pistol. "Don't even touch it," he said. "Use your two fingers and throw it toward me. "The outlaw complied. Lee swung one side of the gate open and seized the handgun. Quickly moving around the wagon, he picked up the rifle and placed them both inside the wagon. He checked the other gate guard; he was gone. Lee took the dead man's pistol and rifle and tossed them into the wagon as well. "Keep your finger in that hole so you don't bleed out, stranger. Give me your other hand." Grabbing it, he put a cuff on it and attached it to the wheel spoke. "Now, don't ya go anywhere, ya hear," he said with a wink.

After noticing the last two gunmen enter the barn, Marshal Lee signaled to a nearby posse member. He climbed over the fence from his position and approached. Gunfire was heard coming from the house. Marshal Lee instructed him to check the ranch house and ensure it was clear. The remaining two men joined Marshal Lee as he positioned himself with his back to the barn. "There's probably a door at the back of the barn. I need one of you two to cover it."

"I got it," said one of the two.

"Any ideas on how to get them out?" the posse member left with Lee asked.

"Let's find out." He gave one of the double barn doors a tug and pulled it open. Bullets slammed into it. "Well, they're still in there."

The marshal called out with a loud voice. "Now listen up, gentlemen. Let me lay it out plain and simple for ya. You two are the last ones standing. Wettin's hitchin' a ride to the big house, and you ain't gettin' a plug nickel outta this mess. Might as well throw up your hands and give it up. "It's my only warning: if'n ya don't throw down your hardware and come out with hands high, we'll burn ya out." He smiled at the man. "How's that?" Two more bullets hit the barn door.

"Sounds like they heard ya."

"That they did," said the marshal. "I caught sight of some sticks and logs for firewood sittin' by the bunkhouse. Why don't ya see if'n ya can rustle up a long stick and snag a sheet or somethin' from the bunkhouse to whip up a torch? We'll give 'em a good scare!"

The posse member sent to the house returned with Sheriff Payne. "The sheriff took out the fella they called Reed," he said. "No one else there."

The marshal smiled at Payne, "Nice work, Sheriff."

Returning from the bunkhouse, the posse member dropped several long branches and rags on the ground. "I also found some wooden matches," hand them to Payne, then helped the marshal build a torch.

"Alright, Payne, light it up." He lit the rag wrapped around the narrow branch, and it flamed. Lee stood back a few feet and gave it a good throw into the barn.

They could hear the two outlaws stumbling around, trying to stomp out the torch while complaining and coughing from the smoke. "Y'all better listen up, boys. There's a whole heap more where that came from. We can keep this showdown rollin' all day and all through the night! At some point, you'll be eatin' embers for breakfast." They could hear the two talking to each other so the marshal butted in. "Ya boys ready for breakfast yet?" he called out.

"Okay, okay, you win, Marshal; we're coming out."

"Fine. Make sure your hands are high. These posse men have itchy fingers."

The two gunmen slowly walked out of the barn. Hands held high. "Well, ain't it mighty fine of y'all to saunter out here in this beautiful weather to join us. Seems like things were heatin' up a tad too much in the barn, wouldn't ya agree?"

Marshal Lee gave Payne a wink. "Well now, that wasn't too tough at all, was it? We'll tie ya fellas to yer horses and scamper on back to town nice and easy-like. Yes siree Bob, we're fixin' to set ya up with some real nice accommodations. You'll each have yer own bunk and two hearty meals a day, all until I can rustle up someone else to take over yer care."

Chapter Twenty-Three

"IT WAS MIDDAY WHEN Rory and Jacob approached the ranch. They paused in the trees and brush lining the hills overlooking the ranch. After dismounting, they observed the ranch. No movement was visible. "Aye, if they be takin' turns keepin' watch over the ranch, I'd be expectin' to see someone wanderin' about or sittin' on the porch, like. It's no' right to leave it all quiet and empty."

"And, I don't see any horses," Jacob added. "They probably put them in the barn if they're down there."

"Oh, I can tell ye for sure and for certain they're down there. I've known men like Wettin, I have. He hails from New York, he does. Spent a fair bit o' time there when I first set me foot in America, I did. They breed naught but murderers and thieves in that place. Aye, many a poor immigrant had to join the gangs to survive, so they did. When the war came, they were either forced or tricked into joinin' the Union, ye know. Those who didn't, well... they were the unsavory lot, the thieves and the gang members. Even those enslaved from the South joined up, lured by the promise of freedom and land, sure enough!

Did your homeland have slavery?" Jacob asked.

"They did, lad. Thanks tae the Vikings, the port of Dublin was a major slave port. It didn't last long. Aye, I am part Scot, but mostly hold tae the Irish. Don't tell anyone," Rory said quietly. Wealthy Scots, however, had their hands in t' plantations, sauntering away with profits from t' West Indian slave trade. The Tobacco Lords were deeply involved in sugar an' cotton production. Back in Scotland, my grandpappy's family were coal miners enslaved tae the mining sites—those collieries and salteries owned by t' well-off. In 1799, Parliament eventually got around tae makin' new laws, but it took a fair number o' years before t' miners finally won their freedom. I tell ye, lad, America is a grand nation, but ye'll find there are scoundrels in every corner. No matter where ye call home, keep ye trust in the Lord. Life's a long road tae tread. He'll guide ye along the way if'n ye let Him."

They watched the ranch for a few moments. "Aye, I'm thinkin' lad," Rory continued. "We should split up, keep 'em guessin' how many o' us there are. Ye should quietly circle round the back o' the house, and I'll gallop up to the front and make meself known. If I can distract 'em, ye can slip in from the rear. What say ye, lad?"

"Good for me."

Jacob mounted his horse and navigated along the backside of the hills. Once in position, he carefully traversed through the garden and trees behind the house. As he approached the house, he glanced up at the window he had climbed out of his first night on the ranch; an idea struck him: he could use that window to enter the house without being seen.

He used the water catch barrel on the side of the porch to stand on and pull himself onto the porch roof. He lifted the sliding window up and climbed inside. He slowly opened the bedroom door and peeked outside. A muffled voice came from below the staircase. He quietly walked over and looked down the stairs. Curby was standing on the porch. A rifle was cradled in his arms. He thought *the others must be in the kitchen*, but he couldn't see them. About that time, Rory came riding in.

"We've got a rider comin' in, boss, Curby said. Jacob moved back to the room, keeping the door open to listen.

Frank Wettin came from the kitchen and stood on the porch beside Curby. Jacob moved from the room back to the top of the staircase to watch.

"It's Rory McDuncan, he's alone."

"Don't bet on it," Wettin said. "I wouldn't be if'n I was him. Keep your eyes open." Both men stepped off the porch and walked out to meet the rider.

It was the opportunity Jacob was waiting for. He went down the stairs and peeked around the corner into the kitchen. Sophia and Alisa were tied to their chairs. Alisa, facing the kitchen entrance, saw Jacob and nearly screamed. Jacob quickly put a finger to his lips as he entered the room. "Be quiet, ladies. Don't say anything. I'm trying to get you out of here. If any shooting starts, drop your chairs to the floor."

Jacob began to untie Sophia when Alisa perked up. "Jacob, they're coming inside," she said hushedly. Jacob's only exit was the screen door in the rear of the kitchen. Exiting, he left it slightly open on purpose. Curby walked in first. He stopped and looked at them. "Something goin' on in here, ladies, what is it?"

"No," said Alisa. "Just waiting for this to be over." He looked around the room. "So, are you planning to let us go anytime soon?" Alisa's mother, Sophia, asked, trying to keep his attention,

Alisa's wrists were chaffed by the coarse rope that bound them. She squirmed as he drew near. Curby's sneer revealed crooked teeth. He leaned in close. "Ain't no one comin' for ya," he softly growled into her ear, his breath sour with whiskey. Turning his head, he noticed the screen door open slightly.

"Has someone been in here?" he asked, moving toward the door.

"Not recently, as far as we know," Alisa said.

"What's this all about?" Wettin said as he walked in behind Rory, a gun to his back.

The women were relieved yet scared. He was alive, and so was Jacob. "Father," Alisa cried out.

"Hush, woman," Wettin said. "Mr. McDuncan, have a seat," seating him opposite Sophia. Rory nodded his head at her and winked at Sophia as he sat. It was a sign that things would be alright.

"I think someone came in," Curby said. "This screen door was closed earlier, and the women couldn't have opened it."

"Well, don't just stand there jawing about it. Help me tie him up, then go take a look around. I've some business to attend to with Rory here. So be quick." Frank Wettin holstered his pistol and leaned against the counter. He tipped his hat up and folded his arms. Ladies, this will all be over soon if Rory does what he's told to do."

Curby walked out the back screen door and glanced in both directions. He wasn't sure which side of the ranch house to walk around first. He drew his six-shooter and turned right. He walked to the house's edge and stopped to peek around it. Nothing was in sight. As he stepped out from the edge of the house, something suddenly fell on him, causing him to sprawl onto the partially dry dirt and grass. Both their handguns slipped from their grasp and landed a few feet away. As he sat up on his knees, Jacob was there to hit him with his fist, but Curby, being experienced, moved his head just in time, and his fist only grazed the ear. He pushed himself forward and grabbed Jacob's legs. Before Curby could push him back, Jacob fell forward onto him. Curby fell to the side with his knees still bent, and on the ground, allowing Jacob to roll free. Both men ran at each other. Curby shoved his knee into Jacob's side. He backed up from the pain but quickly swung himself around in a circle, backhanding Curby as he tried to jump him again. When the backhand hit, it stopped him, causing him to stumble to the side. Jacobs's right followed through, squirting blood from his nose. Curby staggered further to the side but gained his balance, walking in a circle to shake off the blow while holding his nose.

The afternoon sun beat down mercilessly, highlighting the grit on their boots and the sweat on their brows. Curby wiped his face with his sleeve and looked at the blood on it, then at Jacob. Hate and anger were in his eyes. "You're a dead man!"

He clenched his teeth and pulled the pant leg up over his boot, revealing the engraved bone handle knife. "I'm gonna cut ya good!" He snarled, pulling the knife from his boot. Jacob began to circle, but without warning, Curby lunged forward, the blade slicing through the air and leaving a light gash on Jacob's arm. He hissed in pain, instinctively grabbing the wound, while keeping his eyes on his opponent. Curby stepped back with a devious smile. The two men continued to circle in a deadly dance, with Curby feinting with the knife and passing it back and forth between his hands. He suddenly faked a stab, causing Jacob to flinch. Seizing the opportunity, He lunged forward again, but this time Jacob was ready. With lightning-fast reflexes, He turned his body and used his left arm to smash down on Curby's right arm. In one fluid motion, Jacob delivered a powerful kick to the side of Curby's knee.

There was a sickening crack as his knee gave way. Losing his balance and dropping his knife, he fell to the ground, clutching his broken knee, spitting saliva, while screaming vulgarities. He was immobilized. Jacob had no time for him. He wasn't going anywhere unless he crawled or hobbled. Even if he did, he wouldn't get far. Jacob headed for the house, picked up the knife and the two guns along the way. Again, he'd enter the same way he did before, through the bedroom window.

"When Curby gets back, you and I are findin' your property deed," he said to Rory.

"Where's Henry, my ranch foreman?" Rory asked.

"They shot him," Alisa spat out in anger. "He had nothing to do with this. You didn't have to shoot him."

"Doesn't make any difference, lady. He was in the way," he walked over to the screen door. "Where's Curby?"

Wettin was looking out the door when Jacob peeked around the corner. Alisa sat with her back to the screen door, spotting Jacob again. He was making a sign with his hands like it was tipping over. It didn't take her long to do what he was gesturing. She pushed her chair backward and fell against Wettin. He stumbled to the side, and as he did, Sophia, who had been untied but held on to the twine, jumped at Wettin, trying for his holstered gun. The distraction was long enough for Jacob to act. He ran into the kitchen and, sliding across the table, hit Wettin with both feet. Wettin didn't see it coming. He flew back, slamming hard against the screen door, breaking it from its hinges. He and the door crashed onto the porch with a loud thud. Jacob approached him and looked down. The breath had been knocked out of him, leaving him unable to speak. "Nothing to say this time, huh?" Jacob said. He took the Deputy Marshal's badge out of his pocket and pinned it on." You're under arrest." Wettin merely sneered at the badge.

Sophia walked up to Jacob, holding a piece of twine in her hand. Jacob took it and smiled. She then went inside to untie the others while Jacob turned Wettin over and tied his hands behind his back. Helping Wettin to his feet, Jacob said, "Funny, I thought you'd have a lot more colorful things to say. Curby sure did when I beat him down."

He walked Wettin back into the kitchen, Rory had his gun ready. "Rory, if you don't mind, could you take this scoundrel out to the front porch and set him down on one of those fancy rockers you have? I wouldn't want him thinking the McDuncan family is inhospitable. I have another mangy coyote to wrangle out back." Rory just smiled and grabbed Wettin's arm.

Chapter Twenty-Four

Jacob motioned for Alisa to follow him. "Need your help," he said as she followed him around to the side of the house. He pulled Curby's Colt from his waistband and handed it to her. "He's got a bad leg."

"How'd that happen?" she asked.

"Must have tripped or something," Jacob responded. "I've got to help him stand. I need you to cover him while I help, and if he tries anything, anything. You have my permission to shoot him in the other leg," he smiled.

"I was wondering what the purpose of the marshal badge was for," she said with a smile. "To give me permission to shoot him?"

"Well, ya. I 'spose."

"The way I see it, with all the trouble he caused me, I'd shoot him even without your approval, Marshal Long," she teased as Jacob reached down, grabbing the Curby's arm.

"Now, Mr. Curby, I have a lady present. I'd be obliged if you'd keep a civil tongue. By the way, she has permission to shoot you if you don't behave. So, behave please. I'd hate to have to drag you to the front of the house after she shoots you in the other leg. *Comprende?*

Curby looked at Alisa, who was holding the Colt pistol, she had a disdainful expression on her face.

"Ya, I got it," he said.

Curby hobbled to the front porch, his arm around Jacob for support. As much as his mind filled with hate and anger, he wanted to fight Jacob, but his body was too weak from pain. Jacob set him down next to the porch, leaning him against a support beam.

After setting him on the ground, Jacob straightened up and stretched his back. Looking up at the porch, Frank Wettin's hands and legs were tied to the rocking chair. A piece of cloth was tied around his mouth and head.

Rory walked up behind him. "Sophia did that," referring to Wettin being tied to the chair. "She makes a mighty fine knot. Also tired o' the nonsense coming out o' his mouth."

Did you check on Henry?" Jacob asked.

"Aye, poor soul. He was a good man. Didn't deserve it."

Jacob shook his head. "Sometimes a man's just dealt the wrong cards."

Alisa had gone into the house for some cloth to build a splint for Curby's leg. It was painful, but they straightened the leg, placed it on a flat board, and tied a cloth around it to hold it in place. It was all they could do.

A few hours later, Marshal Lee and Sheriff Payne rode in, dismounting at the front porch hitching posts. Rory was seated in a rocker with his rifle. Sheriff Payne paused to look at Wettin and his outlaw holding a glass of lemonade.

"Looks like you've got everything under control," Sheriff Payne said to Rory as the lawmen hitched their horses to the railing.

"Aye, as ye can see. You fellas go on inside, the ladies have some fresh lemonade."

The men sat around the table. "Cali and the posse stayed behind to clean things up at Wettin's ranch. Cali knows the routine, so I put him in charge," Sheriff Payne said. "He'll take the gunmen into town and lock them up. I'll send him back later."

"After they're locked up in the jail," Marshal Lee said, "all three men from the posse will head to Florence to pick up the paddy wagon so we can haul this crew there. They have more cells, and the circuit judge is expected there next week."

Jacob removed the marshal's badge and reached over to hand it to Sheriff Payne. The Marshal put his hand on Jacob's arm. "Why don't ya hold onto that badge for a spell, son. As we rode through these rugged lands, Payne here filled me in on yer story and yer troubles. I reckon you're itching to track down those lowdown scoundrels who wronged ya. But seeing how ya showed restraint and didn' take out those sorry fools loitering outside speaks volumes. You've got grit kid, and the heart of a man the law would be proud to ride alongside.

That badge? I gave it to Sheriff Payne. I told him that if'n a man comes along worth his salt and can get the job done, he should give it to him. It'll open doors and lead ya to places a regular cowboy can't easily git into. More importantly, it just might keep you from deliverin' justice in a fit of rage. Use it wisely. Find those men, bring 'em in, and let justice do its work. Reckon your skills could be just what this rugged territory needs. The good Lord knows we could use more men of your caliber out here.

As for pay, you'll earn two dollars for every criminal you bring in. Plus, six cents for each mile you ride to track 'em down, and ten cents a mile when you haul 'em to court. Those miles count even if you're fetchin' someone from the county jail. You'll be out there in the wilds—might as well make a dollar or two while yer at it."

Jacob pulled his arm back, looked at the badge momentarily, then put it in his pocket.

"I'll get the wagon hitched," Jacob said. "One of them killed Henry, Rory's foreman, and Curby can't ride, so you'll have to take all of them in the wagon."

"Mighty sorry about Henry, Sheriff Payne said to Rory. From what I knew of him, he came from good stock." He stood. "Best be gettin' a move on. If'n ya don't mind, Rory. Just keep their horses and belongings here until we figure things out."

Jacob and Alisa walked alongside the corral, watching the wagon move down the road. Rory had gone to the house to help Sophia repair the busted screen door. "I spose this is goodbye?" she said.

"Let's take a ride," he said.

As the two rode into the hills, Rory and Sophia stood at the door. "I hope that young man stays alive and returns to her," Sophia said, laying her head on Rory's shoulder.

"He's a right clever lad, as crafty and resilient as any coyote. I'll wager ye t' whole farm we'll be seein' him again." The couple returned to the house, closing the door behind them.

Jacob and Alisa dismounted their horses at the top of a high hill, the leather saddles creaking as the wind rustled the leaves in the trees. The sun hung low in the sky, casting a warm, golden glow across the rugged landscape. Alisa couldn't help but watch as Jacob removed his hat and ran a hand through his tousled hair, his eyes scanning the vast open range and appreciating the beauty of the woman beside him.

She adjusted her wide-brimmed hat, the wind tousling her hair while the waning sun cast golden hues through it. Turning away from Jacob, she surveyed the horizon. The scent of juniper, mesquite, and the blooming desert willow, adorned with its magenta flowers, filled the air. Jacob pulled her close as the distant call of a coyote echoed in the hills. They both knew they were in for more adventures in the wild and untamed land of Arizona.

- The End -

Travel the Book

THE FIRST BOOK IN the Superstition Kid series, The Long Road Home, is set around Superior, Arizona. Silver was discovered nearby in 1872, and mining has been a part of Arizona's history since the early 1800s.

The Silver King Mine staked its claim in 1875, the same year the Silver Queen Mine claim was established. Mining camps sprang up near the mines, with the first camp being Happy Hallow, which later evolved into the Silver King camp. It underwent two more name changes, becoming Queen and then Hastings, before finally being named Superior in 1902. Prospectors arrived from all directions as the boom towns expanded. In 1877, another boom town began to develop a few miles from present-day Superior. The Silver King stamp mill was constructed in 1878 to process the silver ore. Later, a smelter was built, and the population grew to around

2,000 people. Initially, the town was called Picketpost, named after the mountain it sat beneath, and it was re-named Pinal City in 1879.

Pinal City or Pinal continued to grow until the price of silver dropped, and the mine closed. The Post Office closed in 1891. Many structures were moved to Superior, and the town became deserted.

In 1879, it's said that Wyatt Earp and his common-law wife, Mattie (Celia Ann "Mattie" Blaylock), traveled with their entourage from Dodge City, Kansas, to Tombstone, Arizona. During their journey, they stopped at Pinal City to try their luck at prospecting. Later, after Wyatt left for California with Josephine, Mattie returned to Pinal in 1881. She passed away and was buried there in 1888.

If you visit Superior, your first stop should be the Bob Jones Museum, where you can learn about the area's rich mining history. If you have any questions or want to learn about events in the area, including the location of Mattie Earp's grave, stop by the Chamber of Commerce.

Explore the legends of Florence, Tombstone, Bisbee, and Douglas, the old Western towns of a bygone era. Travel along Main Street in Florence, featuring deep roots in the Old West with 125 historic adobe and brick buildings in its Historic Downtown. Enjoy eateries and wineries offering Mexican, Greek, and Chinese cuisine.

Look into the past at the Pinal County Historical Museum and the McFarland State Park & Visitors Center.

Discover Tombstone, walk the streets, and experience the shootouts as the cowboys and miners did. Become a spectator at the O.K. Corral, or visit an original bar and dance hall at the Bird Cage Theater.

Continue your journey at Bisbee's Copper Queen Mine and the Bisbee Mining & Historical Museum. The town was built around the smelter for the Bisbee mines.

Douglas is rich in border history. One notable landmark is the historic Gadsden Hotel, which opened in 1907 and has hosted many famous actors, cowboys, and outlaws. Be sure to visit the Douglas Grand Theater as well; at the time of its opening, it was the largest theater between Los Angeles and San Antonio.

East of Superior, you'll want to visit Globe. Established in 1871 and situated within the Tonto National Forest, this historic town offers historic hotels, Mexican dining, art galleries, and shops to explore.

Explore this region's early mining era, its geological history, and Indigenous folklore. Immerse yourself in the charm of old Western towns to truly experience the past.

The United States offers a wealth of majestic beauty and rich history that'll provide a lifetime of adventure.

Take a drive today and discover what you've been missing. I promise, you won't be disappointed!